LATE, LATE IN THE EVENING

Gladys Maude Winifred Mitchell – or 'The Great Gladys' as Philip Larkin called her – was born in 1901, in Cowley in Oxfordshire. She graduated in history from University College London and in 1921 began her long career as a teacher. She studied the works of Sigmund Freud and attributed her interest in witchcraft to the influence of her friend, the detective novelist Helen Simpson.

Her first novel, *Speedy Death*, was published in 1929 and introduced readers to Beatrice Adela Lestrange Bradley, the heroine of a further sixty six crime novels. She wrote at least one novel a year throughout her career and was an early member of the Detection Club, alongside Agatha Christie, G.K Chesterton and Dorothy Sayers. In 1961 she retired from teaching and, from her home in Dorset, continued to write, receiving the Crime Writers' Association Silver Dagger in 1976. Gladys Mitchell died in 1983.

ALSO BY GLADYS MITCHELL

Speedy Death
The Mystery of a Butcher's Shop
The Longer Bodies
The Saltmarsh Murders
Death and the Opera
The Devil at Saxon Wall
Dead Men's Morris
Come Away, Death
St Peter's Finger
Printer's Error
Hangman's Curfew
When Last I Died
Laurels Are Poison
The Worsted Viper
Sunset Over Soho
My Father Sleeps
The Rising of the Moon
Here Comes a Chopper
Death and the Maiden
Tom Brown's Body
Groaning Spinney
The Devil's Elbow
The Echoing Strangers
Merlin's Furlong
Watson's Choice
Faintley Speaking
Twelve Horses and the Hang-man's Noose
The Twenty-Third Man
Spotted Hemlock
The Man Who Grew Tomatoes
Say It With Flowers
The Nodding Canaries
My Bones Will Keep
Adders on the Heath
Death of the Delft Blue
Pageant of a Murder
The Croaking Raven
Skeleton Island
Three Quick and Five Dead
Dance to Your Daddy
Gory Dew
Lament for Leto
A Hearse on May-Day
The Murder of Busy Lizzie
Winking at the Brim
A Javelin for Jonah
Convent on Styx
Late, Late in the Evening
Noonday and Night
Fault in the Structure
Wraiths and Changelings
Mingled With Venom
The Mudflats of the Dead
Nest of Vipers
Uncoffin'd Clay
The Whispering Knights
Lovers, Make Moan
The Death-Cap Dancers
The Death of a Burrowing Mole
Here Lies Gloria Mundy
Cold, Lone and Still
The Greenstone Griffins
The Crozier Pharaohs
No Winding-Sheet

VINTAGE MURDER MYSTERIES

With the sign of a human skull upon its back and a melancholy shriek emitted when disturbed, the Death's Head Hawkmoth has for centuries been a bringer of doom and an omen of death - which is why we chose it as the emblem for our Vintage Murder Mysteries.

Some say that its appearance in King George III's bedchamber pushed him into madness. Others believe that should its wings extinguish a candle by night, those nearby will be cursed with blindness. Indeed its very name, *Acherontia atropos*, delves into the most sinister realms of Greek mythology: Acheron, the River of Pain in the underworld, and Atropos, the Fate charged with severing the thread of life.

The perfect companion, then, for our Vintage Murder Mysteries sleuths, for whom sinister occurrences are never far away and murder is always just around the corner …

GLADYS MITCHELL

Late, Late in the Evening

VINTAGE BOOKS
London

Published by Vintage 2014

2 4 6 8 10 9 7 5 3 1

First published in Great Britain by Michael Joseph Ltd in 1976

Vintage
Random House, 20 Vauxhall Bridge Road,
London SW1V 2SA

www.vintage-books.co.uk

Addresses for companies within The Random House Group Limited can be found at: www.randomhouse.co.uk/offices.htm

The Random House Group Limited Reg. No. 954009

A CIP catalogue record for this book is available from the British Library

ISBN 9780099583929

Printed and bound in Great Britain by Clays Ltd, St Ives plc

Part One: Evidence

CHAPTER I

Margaret and Kenneth

The village looks different now. It has become an urban overspill area. Factories have grown up, a motorway runs nearby and what used to be open country, including Lye Hill and the vast common we called The Marsh, has been given over to council houses and tall blocks of flats. Even my grandfather's four or five arable acres have gone and in their place there is a housing estate of small, neat bungalows, each with its patch of front lawn and small back garden.

In my early childhood the village occupied only two streets and these were at right-angles to one another. On the road which ran steeply uphill to the manor house my grandfather had built two imposing semi-detached villas. They had flights of broad stone steps up to the front door, basement kitchens which opened into very large, non-basement sculleries at the back and they were furnished with back and front staircases. Grandfather and his widowed daughter, our Aunt Lally, occupied the villa with the passion-flower plant at the side of the front door and the other house, which had trails of periwinkles down the side entrance, belonged to Uncle Arthur and Aunt Kirstie. Both houses had long back gardens with end-gates which opened on to grandfather's small-holding.

My mother and father, who had shared grandfather's house when they were first married, moved to a London suburb after Kenneth was born, so neither he nor I regarded ourselves as natives of the village, although we spent our summers there.

When it was term-time we attended the village school. I remember very little about it except that children of all ages were taught in a large room which had been built as a chapel and that (I suppose because of the age-range of the twenty or so pupils) we older ones spent a great deal of our time in an exercise called Transcription. This meant that, in our best handwriting, we copied chunks of history, geography and poetry out of dog-eared, grimy, tattered text-books. I cannot remember that our work was ever tested or corrected, but at any rate it put no strain on the intellect.

When Saturday came there was our pocket-money to spend. Where the bingo hall now stands there used to be old Mother Honour's little post-office and general store and where Miss Summers had her shop, that and a few cottages have been pulled down and a supermarket built.

In our day we usually patronised Mother Honour. She was a shrewish old lady who detested children, but if the brass bowl on her pair of scales hovered uncertainly, she would (grudgingly) drop in another sweet, whereas Miss Summers, who sold bread and buns as well as confectionery, faced with the same problem, would be content to leave the scales wavering always slightly to her advantage, never to ours. She was gushing, blonde and plump, and was said to have designs on the baker who came from the town to deliver the loaves which she sold to the villagers.

The only reason we ever gave her our custom was that she sold so-called brandy balls, hard, dark-brown, glistening, strongly-flavoured sweets which Mother Honour did not stock. They could be pouched in the cheek and made to last a good long time. I think the two shopkeepers must have had some kind of gentleman's agreement not to duplicate their stock, so that there should be no poaching on one another's preserves. 'Live and let live' seemed to be their motto, and although neither woman was conspicuously prosperous, nor did either of them fail to make ends meet.

We had several sets of relations in and around the village, but when we played with other children it was not with our cousins, who were mostly older than we were, but under the leadership and guidance, not to say protection and patronage, of a biggish girl known as Our Sarah. We were pleased to belong to her band, although she bossed us about, as she did all the other children. I always felt, though, that Kenneth and I were mere hangers-on, for she never addressed us by our names. It was always: 'Hoy, you young Oi say! Come on out o' that brook. Your auntie's 'olleren for you,' or, 'Hoy you young Oi say! Tuck them trousis up 'oigher, else you be goen to get 'em wet, and then you won't arf get an 'oiden.'

The brook was our chief plaything. It conveniently ran alongside The Marsh at the bottom of our grandfather's acres, so that Kenneth and I could cross on to The Marsh by way of an iron gate and a broad plank bridge, both of them grandfather's property, whereas all the other children had to walk to the end of the village and cross by a bridge which spanned a culvert. It never occurred either to us or to them that they should take the short cut across grandfather's land. Perhaps they, like ourselves, went in awe of him, for he was in all respects the village patriarch and owned more than half its cottages.

Apart from giving easy access to the brook, his grounds were a paradise for young children. There were raspberry canes and currant bushes which we were allowed to plunder as we pleased. There were pigs, ducks, chickens, sometimes a calf and there was also a stable containing a vicious mare named Polly whom we were forbidden to approach.

Best of all there were Uncle Arthur's whippets, Floss and Vicky. Floss was a graceful fawn-coloured animal, a bitch in every sense, for she had a most unpredictable temper, loving you one minute and, for no apparent reason, viciously snapping at you the next.

Vicky, on the other hand, was a liver-coloured little love, the sweetest-natured creature that ever allowed young children to dress her up in their sweaters, almost smother her with clumsy caresses and take her for walks with an undignified piece of string tied to her collar. Her affection for us was boundless and was as sincere as it was touching.

We had little in common with the ducks or chickens. The

latter pecked us when we turned them off their roosting boxes to collect the eggs, and we were nauseated by the former when we saw two of them disputing possession of a frog. We rescued the frog and Kenneth took it over to the well, but in dropping it in he slipped and went in, too—luckily feet first. He managed to clutch the edge of the brickwork and I held on to him and bellowed for help. Fortunately this happened to be at hand in the person of Uncle Arthur, who was boiling tiny jacket potatoes in an outside copper for the pigs. As a reward for saving Kenneth's life I claimed and was given as many of the pigs' delicious potatoes as I could eat.

We took all our meals at Aunt Kirstie's. She was a better cook than Aunt Lally and a much more indulgent person than grandfather, who found children a nuisance at the table because he said we chattered. We would have liked to stay altogether with Aunt Kirstie and Uncle Arthur, but two of their upstairs rooms were given over permanently to a lodger, a snuff-taking, silent old gentleman named Mr Ward, who (so we heard) was some connexion of the Kempsons up at the manor house. So far as I remember, he never addressed a word to us, but sometimes we would come upon him out on The Marsh or at the foot of Lye Hill near the sheepwash. He would be digging, but for what purpose we had no idea.

He was not the only person in the village about whom we speculated. Another was Mrs Grant. She was always to be found seated on the doorstep of her respectable little cottage and she never seemed to cease rocking herself to and fro and declaiming to anybody who was passing, 'I hab de ague, bery bad, bery bad.' She claimed to be Maltese and the widow of an English sailor. The village children used to mock her. We were neither old enough, nor courageous enough, to take her side against their tauntings, but at least we never joined in the teasing. I think now that she was not a Maltese, but an African. She was certainly darker-skinned than the Maltese I have seen since, and her lamentations had an air of African fatality about them. The village children would shout,

'Black-pudden! Black-pudden!' as they passed her; but, as Kenneth said to me:

'Black-puddings are very nice, and I expect she'd be nice, too, if we ever got to know her.' (We did, in a way, later on because of the murders.)

Further down the road lived the Widow Winter, whose sole occupation, once she had whitened her doorstep, seemed to be to spy on the rest of the village from behind a barricade of flowering plants. She believed, I suppose, that these hid her prying eyes from passers-by while she watched from her parlour window, hour after hour, the comings and goings of her neighbours. I have no doubt that she knew exactly how often the people across the street washed their lace curtains, how long Miss Summers spent in her daily dallyings with the baker and exactly what was in everybody's string bag when people came back from their weekend shopping at the Co-op in the town. Everybody did the big weekend shopping at the Co-op because of something mysterious called the divvy.

From these Saturday expeditions we could always expect a pleasant surprise on Sunday mornings, for on the bedside table in Aunt Kirstie's room would be sugar mice in pink or white with tiny black eyes and their tails made out of string, or there might be sugar pigs or a bar of chocolate cream. Another joy was bathtime. At that age we were bathed in the large zinc tub Aunt Kirstie used for her laundry. There was no bathroom and the stone-floored scullery was considered too cold, even in summer, so, as there was always a fire in the kitchen for cooking, we were bathed in front of that. I remember that there was some special soap (said to have been made in Japan) which floated, and when we had been dried we had a glorious toasting in front of the fire.

Almost opposite our two villas there were two semi-detached cottages. They were inhabited by a brother and sister who had quarrelled many years before we were born and who never spoke to one another. They had long, beautifully-tended gardens which bordered the road and the two old people were at war every fruit-picking season with the village children, for the old lady grew strawberries and the old man had a particularly fine pear-tree. I do not believe Kenneth and I would ever have joined in the raids but, in any case, there was no temptation for us, as grandfather grew more fruit than we could eat or the aunts could make into jam.

At the end of the village, opposite Mother Honour's shop, was a tumble-down cottage where a hermit had once lived. The cottage was in the last stages of disrepair and he himself had been ragged and indescribably filthy. After he died it was discovered that he had pulled up all the floorboards and must have used them for fuel. So far as anybody could make out, all he had to live on were the stale loaves from Miss Summers' shop. Her one and only charitable action was to leave any left-overs on her doorstep overnight. As they had always disappeared by morning, it was assumed that the hermit collected them under cover of darkness and ate them.

Outside the village, but still in a sense of it, as were the people at the manor house, there were the gypsies who, every summer, had an encampment at the top of Lye Hill. Lye Hill was forbidden territory to Kenneth and me. The reason given to us by Aunt Lally (she who looked after our grandfather) was that the gypsies kidnapped small children and sold them as slaves, but the real reason (as I found out much later) was that Lye Hill was an extension of Lovers' Lane, which was also forbidden territory to us because the villagers did all their coupling in summer in the open air.

To speak to Old Sukie, the gypsy who, now and again, walked into the town with a male companion to sell clothes-pegs and paper flowers, was the favourite village 'dare' and, so far as I know, had no takers until Kenneth volunteered to waylay the so-called witch and pass the time of day with her. As my pride and my sense of responsibility would not allow me to leave him to his fate, I went along, although most unwillingly and with great trepidation, to support him. Day after day we waited on the drove road which ran alongside the brook and at last, while the village children watched from a safe distance, Kenneth's opportunity came.

When he saw the gypsies approaching, Sukie with a large wicker basket on her arm and the man slouching along beside her, Kenneth pulled his cap out of his pocket, put it on his head and then, as the gypsies came almost up to us, he raised it politely and said, 'Good morning, madam. It's a very nice morning, isn't it?'

The man muttered something and did not shorten his stride but, to my alarm, Old Sukie stopped. However, she smiled and said, 'Good day to you, my little gentleman. Wear a flower for me, then, my lover. You have a lucky face.' With that, and with Kenneth standing his ground while I drew back a pace, she picked a paper flower from her basket and handed it to him before she strode on after her man. Although she was always known as Old Sukie, she could not have been more than thirty years of age. She was a striking-looking woman in her gypsy fashion, and she carried herself like a queen.

The dark man with her—her husband, I suppose, although Our Sarah told us, with a great air of mystery and with what I now realise was a lascivious gleam in her eye, that if they were married at all it was 'only over the tongs'—was a furtive-looking fellow, but lithe and tigerish. He was tall for a gypsy and his slouching stride covered the ground with an effortless unhurried, prowling effect which was more frightening to us even than the reputation Sukie had of being a witch. His silence, too, and his apparent disregard of our presence, carried their own menace.

Soon after our first acquaintance, if one may call it that, with the gypsies, Kenneth and I gained a new companion. This was a puckish-looking, unusually tall young boy wearing a blue shirt and grey-flannel shorts who came barefoot down the road one day and found us about to take Vicky for a walk. He stopped and spoke, with an intonation so unlike our own that we were somewhat abashed, for we recognised him, in spite of his workaday costume, tousled hair and bare feet, as what Aunt Lally called 'one of the gentry'.

'Hullo. Is that your dog?' he asked.

'My uncle's,' I explained.

'It's going to rain.'

This *non sequitur* nonplussed me.

'How do you know?' I demanded. Instead of replying, he asked,

'Has your aunt—I suppose you've got an aunt if you've got

an uncle—has she a good big tin bath? A really big one, I mean.'

'There *is* one, yes,' said Kenneth. 'She does the washing in it.' He did not add that we were bathed in it, too.

'Oh, good,' said the boy. 'I should think a lot of water comes down this hill when it rains.' He wriggled a big toe into the soft surface of the road. 'Nothing but sand,' he said. 'Tell you what. I'll wait for you while you take the dog out, then you borrow this tin bath of your aunt's and a spade or a trowel, see? Then we sink the bath in the middle of the road and the rainwater fills it up and we paddle. All right?'

'Suppose somebody wants to bring a cart along, or the doctor comes by on his horse?' said Kenneth.

'In the rain? Oh, they won't. Off you go with your dog and don't be long. As soon as the dog has done what it has to do, back you come, do you see? And hurry it up a bit.'

'Who do you think you're talking to?' said Kenneth. 'Besides, we wouldn't be given the bath to play with, *or* be allowed to paddle in the road in the rain. You must be daft!'

'What *can* we do, then?' asked the boy, deflated quite obviously by this spirited comment.

'If you'd like to come with us, you can,' I replied, 'then when we come back you could see our pigs and have a go on our swing in the cartshed.'

'I'd rather paddle.'

'Well, look,' said Kenneth. 'I dare say Aunt Kirstie would let us paddle in the bath if we had it in the scullery. There's a big enamel jug in there to fill it. It would be quicker than waiting for the rain. Or there's the brook. That's better still for paddling.'

'What brook?'

'Come with us, and we'll show you.'

'All right. What's your name?'

'Kenneth Clifton. This is my sister Margaret.'

'How do you do? I am Lionel Kempson-Conyers. We only began the summer vac. yesterday and already I'm bored. The house'—he jerked his head towards the top of the hill—'is going to be full up with people and nobody's got any time for me. My parents have gone back to France. They live there mostly. They'll bring back my sister, who's at finishing-school over there. There isn't even a pony to ride here. It's just too plain boring for words. Do you play cricket?'

'Not really,' replied Kenneth. 'Can you box?'

'No, worse luck. We don't take boxing at school until we're eleven and I'm only nine.'

This surprised us because of his height, but all Kenneth said was, 'I'm eight and my sister's ten.'

'Can *she* box?'

'Of course. Our Uncle Arthur teaches both of us.'

'How decent for you.' By this time we were strolling along, with Vicky on her bit of string, towards the end of the village. By the time Aunt Kirstie had tea ready we were back from our walk and were taking turns on the swing. At Lionel Kempson-Conyers' suggestion, we were having a competition to see who could be the first to kick a bit off the cartshed roof, which was made of sheets of corrugated iron.

Lionel stayed to tea that day. After that, more often than not, he came down the hill into the village to play with us. Our Sarah was contemptuous of our new acquaintance.

'Hoy, you young Oi say,' she remarked bitterly one morning before Lionel came along, 'who be that there young Oi say as you be goen weth nowadays?'

'He's a friend of ours,' said Kenneth, 'but, truly, Our Sarah, we'd rather be with you.'

'So you says. A lettle bet of a lah-di-dah, ennee? Seems loike I heered hem talken to you t'other day loike the gentry talks, and that's talk as Oi don't 'old weth, nor moi dad neether.'

'I think he's a nobleman's son. His name is Lionel Kempson-Conyers. Wouldn't you call that a nobleman's name? And I think he goes to boarding-school. He calls it a prep. school and they get the cane there ever so often,' said Kenneth. 'I'd hate to go there.'

'You ever had the cane, you young Oi say?'

'No,' said Kenneth, 'I shouldn't allow it.'

'What 'ud ee do, then?'

'Hit the teacher in the stomach, which is pretty effective, though it's against the Queensberry rules. That's if it was a man. I should take the cane away and break it, if it was a woman,' said Kenneth. Sarah eyed him.

'Fierce as a maggot, beant ee?' she said sardonically. 'Well, Oi tells ee *thes*: you ded oughter watch out, 'cos ef thes 'ere young Oi say be one o' them Kempson lot, moi dad *do* say as they ain't no better 'an they should be.'

'What does that mean?'

'Never you moind what et means at your age. You'll know all about et when you be older.'

'Our Sarah,' said Kenneth earnestly, 'Lionel hates all his relations up at the big house. Will you let him join the band? He isn't really lah-di-dah, I promise you. Can't he come to the sheepwash with us?'

No embargo was ever placed on our playing in and beside the brook, but the sheepwash at the foot of Lye Hill was supposed to be out of bounds to us. It was a part of the brook which had been artificially deepened and its sides had been shored up, but in our time it was never used for its original purpose, for there were no longer any sheep on The Marsh or on the hill. Whereas the brook itself was nowhere more than a few inches deep, the sheepwash which it fed had a depth of about a foot at its shallowest and almost four feet of water in the deepest part. We often went there in spite of prohibitions, for it made a splendid pool, and there was a game of seeing how far you could wade in without actually wetting your clothes. Kenneth slipped over once and got himself soaked. Our Sarah squeezed him as dry as she could and then ran him all the way home and delivered him to Aunt Kirstie with the remark, ''Ere be your young Oi say, missus. Fell over en the brook and wet hesself. 'Tweren't hes fault, Oi don't reckon. Our Ern gev hem a lettle bet of a shove, loike. Oi'll sort Our Ern when Oi cotches up weth hem.'

I remember that we debated earnestly that night when we got to bed—for at that time we still shared a room—whether or not we ought to confess that it was in the sheepwash, and not in the brook proper, that Kenneth had had his ducking.

However, we agreed, with smug sanctimoniousness, that it would be hard lines on Our Sarah if we let her down after she had told such gallant fibs on our behalf. 'Besides,' added Kenneth, 'Aunt Kirstie might make us promise *on our honour* not to go near the sheepwash again, and that would be very awkward.'

'And, after all, the sheepwash *is* the brook,' I said, 'when you come right down to it.' (Even at the time I was slightly ashamed of this piece of sophistry.)

'It was good of Our Sarah to blame it on Ern, because he wasn't even there,' said Kenneth. 'We can't make her out to be a—to tell stories, can we?' (The word *liar* was on the forbidden list in our vocabulary; so was *hell.* As for *damn* and *bloody,* these were not words we ever heard except from the lips of drunken men, and even then they filled us with pity and terror, as being expressions which even God, powerful though we knew Him to be, could neither excuse nor forgive.)

It is no wonder that in some ways we were a couple of sanctimonious little prigs. Our nightly prayers, for example, were always said downstairs quite often in front of a circle of admiring relatives of whom Aunt Lally, although not the most loving, was the most sentimental. She would exclaim, when the recitation of our little piece was over: 'Don't they say them words pretty!' Then she would present each of us with a biscuit out of a special tin and we would go up to bed feeling satisfied with our performance, although a little scornful of our aunt, who had not realised what an artistic bit of eye-wash it had been.

CHAPTER 2

Mr Ward

As usual we enjoyed ourselves down at the sheepwash. Lionel asked how deep it was.

'Deep enough to drownd two loike you, you young Oi say,' replied Our Sarah. Lionel went over to the hedge which bordered Lye Hill and broke off a long stick. He lay on his stomach and tested the depth of the water at the deepest part, but the stick did not reach the bottom.

'Oh, good!' he said. 'If you girls would go away, we boys could have a good dip.'

'That ud be rude,' said Our Sarah. 'You ent got your bathers weth ee.'

'Oh, no, it wouldn't be rude. Of course it wouldn't. We always bathe naked at school.'

'Oi tell ee et's rude.'

'Then you're an ignorant peasant.'

'No, she isn't,' said Kenneth. 'It depends on the point of view. And it's very ignorant of you to talk about peasants when you only mean villagers.'

'Can you swim?' asked Lionel. We had noticed that he always retreated in some way or other when he was contradicted or challenged. We also soon found out that he blabbed, so we did not tell him much.

'He's a bit of a coward, isn't he?' said Kenneth to me, later. 'I mean, I'm a year younger than him and not nearly as tall. He ought to have busted me one. I quite expected it.'

'I expect he's been bullied at school,' I replied. In the boys' books we got from the library when we were at home there was always bullying at boarding-schools. 'It would make anybody a coward if they were always being bullied.'

'Father gave me sixpence last year for punching Tom Speery when he tried it on.'

'Because Tom was older and bigger than you. I wish I could earn sixpence that way.'

'I split it with you, didn't I?'

'It's not the same as earning it.'

'Do you suppose Lionel gets much pocket-money?'

'We've never been with him when he spent any.'

'Perhaps he's a miser as well as a coward, and I know he blabs about things you'd think ought to be a secret.'

'Some people say the old man who died—that tramp who had the tumble-down place at the bottom of the hill—some people say *he* was a miser.'

'I wonder! If he was, he could have left a hidden treasure—money, you know, or jewels.'

'In that cottage?'

'Well, he might have done. Such things have been known. Maybe he left a code message to say where he buried it.'

'Or a map, like *Treasure Island*.'

'We might go and see.'

'Would we take Lionel?'

'Why? It's our idea, not his. Besides, he's been to tea with us twice, but he's never asked us back.'

'Perhaps he can't. Besides, what would we do in a big house like his? There might be all sorts of difficulties. Suppose we spilt our tea or knocked something over?'

'It wouldn't matter. Rich children always have tea in the schoolroom or the nursery. They never have meals with their parents downstairs.'

'Anyway, what about the old man's treasure?'

We decided to try our luck at the cottage without Lionel's assistance. Breakfast for us was at eight and we always had it without Mr Ward, who did not often come downstairs until ten. Aunt Kirstie was never known to grumble at having to cook a separate breakfast for him. He seldom appeared at lunch, either. Our Sarah told us that she reckoned he got his mid-day meal at the pub and added the further information that he was a dirty old man.

'I wouldn't call him dirty, would you?' Kenneth said.

'He takes snuff and blows his nose rather a lot,' I replied. 'Perhaps that's what she meant.' It was eight o'clock on a fine Saturday morning. We were surprised to find a used cup and saucer and a greasy plate in Mr Ward's place at table when we came down.

'He came early for his breakfast,' Aunt Kirstie explained. 'Got to go out and do a bit more digging, he told me. Well, what's it to be? Bacon and egg and a bit of black-pudding?'

'And fried bread,' said Kenneth. We never took long to eat our meals, but that Saturday morning we were even quicker than usual. We had exchanged glances when we heard that Mr Ward had had his breakfast at least two hours earlier than usual and had announced that he was going out to dig, and the same thought was in both our minds. Mr Ward must have had the same idea as we had. He must have got wind of treasure buried under the floor of the hermit's cottage. There could be no other explanation.

We cleared our plates, thanked God for our good breakfast, *Amen,* and rushed out of doors. Breakfast was always in Aunt Kirstie's big basement kitchen, so the quickest way out was through the scullery into the back garden and up the sloping side-walk.

Mr Ward was not at the hermit's cottage. He was shovelling away among Uncle Arthur's gladioli. We were delighted to see him there, although we thought Uncle Arthur would be less pleased.

'We'll go to the cottage,' said Kenneth, 'and have a good look round for any clues to the treasure before he gets there.'

'I believe we ought to tell Aunt Kirstie what Mr Ward is up to,' I said. 'It's a pity Uncle Arthur isn't at home.'

'She may not like to interfere. He pays for his board and lodging, you know.'

We debated the point as we walked towards the road and

by the time we got round to the front of the house I had gained my way, so we went back again to tell Aunt Kirstie that Mr Ward was digging up the gladioli, but, when we turned in at grandfather's big gates, Mr Ward had found a new place to dig.

He was in the middle of grandfather's big chicken run and was busy there scooping away with his spade, while the hens were squawking and fluttering and the Rhode Island Red cock, always the bravest bird, was making little, abortive rushes at Mr Ward's elastic-sided boots.

'A good thing we did come back,' said Kenneth, as Mr Ward took a swipe at the cock with his spade. 'Come on, quick!' We ran towards him and Kenneth bravely shouted out: 'Mr Ward! Mr Ward! Aunt Kirstie wants you!' Then we went in at the garden gate to find Aunt Kirstie for ourselves. When she came with us, however, having waited to take off her apron and tidy her hair—but really, I think, to pluck up courage before she tackled Mr Ward, of whom we knew she was somewhat in awe because of his superior social status—he was no longer in the chicken run, so off we went towards the cottage.

At that time we had to go down the village street to get there, although we found a better way later. However, just as we were opposite Mrs Grant's house—she was seated on her doorstep as usual, rocking herself and moaning about her ague—a man on horseback caught up with us and reined in. We recognised him as Doctor Matters' assistant. His name was Doctor Tassall.

'You youngsters want to earn a penny?' he asked.

'Each?' asked Kenneth. The young doctor laughed.

'All right, Shylock my son, a penny each,' he said.

'To do what?' I asked.

'To post a letter in the box on Mrs Honour's wall. I've got to go in and have a look at this patient, and I don't want to miss the post.'

We noticed then that Mrs Grant had retreated into her cottage. The doctor dismounted, handed Kenneth the letter and a penny, gave me a penny, tied his horse up to Mrs Grant's railings and went into the cottage. We walked on down the hill to post the letter in Old Mother Honour's pillar-box. It was not really a pillar-box, just a post-office opening in the shop wall with the times of collection on it. Of course we read the envelope before we posted it.

'Miss A. Kempson-Conyers,' I said. 'Hill Manor House, Hill, Oxon. It must be to one of Lionel's relations.'

'He said he'd got an older sister,' said Kenneth. We put the letter in the box and then had a short discussion on how best to lay out the pennies we had been given. We had our usual Saturday pennies with us as well, and such riches merited careful thought in the spending. In the end we agreed to tackle the treasure-hunt first and lay out our augmented income on the way home.

'We shall have to watch out,' I said. 'Always a crowd of hangers-on when they know we've got anything to spend.' This sounds a mean kind of remark, but we had learned the hard way and had grown cagey about sharing our sweets with anybody but one another. There were some rapacious characters in the village.

'Bloody cormorants!' said Kenneth. 'Heard a man say it when Uncle Arthur took us to the covered market,' he added, seeing my look of horrified admiration. 'Shan't say it again, I promise you, but some of the big ones are.'

I stored up the phrase for use in our London school playground and we crossed the road and approached the decrepit cottage. Away on The Marsh we could hear the village children at play. Inside the cottage another sound was being made. We halted and listened. It was plain enough what was happening there. Nobody could mistake the sound of a pickaxe.

'We've been out-smarted,' muttered Kenneth. 'Let's sneak up and see who it is.'

The cottage had no front door. That, like the floor-boards. had disappeared long since and, from previous peering through the iron railings which shut off the back garden of the cottage from grandfather's land, we knew that all the other doors—the kitchen, the woodshed and the earth-closet—had gone the same way. We also knew that the cottage was 'two up and two down'. The stairs, however, were now completely unsafe, although Our Ern, a foxy, freckled little boy as thin as a skinned rabbit and as active as a squirrel, had once climbed up them as a 'dare' and had endured a punishing punch-up with Our Sarah afterwards for risking his neck, because part of the staircase had come down with him when he descended.

All the cottages on that side of the street had narrow back gardens which abutted on to grandfather's land and, as he owned all of them, grandfather had seen to it that they had no back entrances, so that the tenants could not trespass on his small-holding. The hermit's cottage was no exception. I once heard Aunt Lally ask grandfather why he had not turned the hermit out, repaired the cottage and let it, but all he said was, 'Live and let live, my lass. Remember what happened to Dives, who also had a beggar at his gate.'

'They're in the front room,' said Kenneth, 'whoever it is. Let's go round the back.'

'We can't,' I said. 'Not to sneak in, I mean. We can't get over that iron fence, and, if we did get over, we might not be able to get back.'

'Oh, that's all right. There's a ladder in the cartshed. We could use that.'

'To get over? Well, perhaps, but we still couldn't get back without lifting the ladder across, and I don't believe we could manage it. The ladder's too long and heavy.'

'We'll worry about that later on.'

'We could get in over the side wall,' I said, eyeing the only part of the property which grandfather kept in repair to mark the boundary of his jurisdiction, for the cottage was the last one in the road, 'if it wasn't for all that broken glass on top.'

'Yes, that's no good. Well, come on. Let's get that ladder. We'd better go in through grandfather's big gates again, not the side entrance. We don't want anybody to see us. There might be questions asked.'

The big gates were those through which we had passed to get to the chicken run and through which, at one time, when he and Polly the horse were younger, our grandfather had driven the wagon to market. They were always wide open nowadays and nobody except ourselves used them. We trudged up the hill, darted in through the big gates to the small-holding and took the broad path to the well. Here we turned at right-angles for the cartshed and found the ladder. It was long and heavy. In the end it proved too much for us.

'Oh, blow!' said Kenneth. 'Now what do we do?'

'If it's a workman to do some repairs, he'll knock off at twelve,' I said. 'Let's go and spend our money and wait for him to go.'

'It's *hours* before twelve. I vote we snake in by the front door and see who's there. If it's a workman he'll only tell us to hop it.'

'But I don't believe it *is* a workman,' I said. 'I heard Uncle Arthur tell Aunt Kirstie that all the place was fit for was to come down and that he was sorry for the chaps who had to do the job because the bugs would be worse than a London slum. Anyway, it's Saturday. They wouldn't start a job like that on a Saturday.'

'Then it's Mr Ward. He might get waxy if we spied on him.'

'All right, then, let's spend. Brandy balls or Old Mother Honour?'

'We've got enough for both.' We stopped at Miss Summers' shop. It was not a real shop, as Old Mother Honour's was. By that I mean it had been built as an ordinary house, but Miss Summers' father, who had had it before her, had altered the front window and made it into a big, square bay with a broad shelf behind on which were loaves and buns and a couple of jars of sweets to show that she sold those as well.

As we were looking in at the window, Our Ern came up behind us.

'Hullo! Spenden?' he asked covetously. 'Me, Oi be saven up for the fair.'

'Oh, so are we,' said Kenneth. 'How much have you got?'

'Two shellen and tuppence. Oi ben sellen buckets o' dung. Our Sarah, her got near enough foive bob. Her ben taken lettle babies out. Sometoimes her gets gev as much as a sex-pence for that.'

'Where does she get the babies from?' (Kenneth knew that nobody in the village would give twopence, let alone sixpence, for pushing a baby out in its perambulator.)

'En the town of a Saturday afternoon when her's done out our bedrooms.'

'And where do you get the manure?'

'At the stables where the College gents keeps their 'orses. Oi reckons to 'ave foive bob, too, come the fair.'

'*You* could take babies out, couldn't you?' said Kenneth, when Our Ern had gone.

'No, I couldn't. I hate babies,' I said. 'And you wouldn't be allowed to collect buckets of manure, so you needn't think any more about it.'

'I could get it from old Polly's stable, but I wouldn't know where to sell it.'

'Old Polly bites and kicks. Look, the coast's clear. Let's buy the brandy balls.'

We did this, and bought four ounces between us instead of two ounces each.

'That way,' said Kenneth, when we left the shop, 'she can only cheat us out of one brandy ball, not two.' I did not need this explanation, as the manoeuvre was one we had used before. The only snag was that sometimes, when it came to the divvying up, there was an odd instead of an even number of brandy balls. However, we were accustomed to solve this problem by taking turns at sucking the extra sweet. On arrival at Mother Honour's we saw a couple of the village children coming towards us, so we did not stop, but strolled on as though we were going on to The Marsh.

'Ent you got nothen to spend, then?' asked one child, with a sneer. 'Thought you was rech!'

'Saving up for the fair,' said Kenneth promptly. 'What about you?'

'Oh,' said the other, 'us too an' all. Bet you ent got as much as Oi 'ave.'

'Six shillings,' said Kenneth, lying, of course.

'Garn! Oi don't believe et! Let's see et, then.'

'You'll see it when the time comes.'

'Foight you for et!'

'You don't think I carry it about with me, do you? My uncle is minding it for me. You can fight *him* for it, if you like.' We strolled on. As we turned the corner I glanced back.

'O.K. They've gone into their house,' I said. As we came out of Mother Honour's we saw Mr Ward come out of the hermit's cottage. Kenneth pulled me back inside the shop, so Mr Ward did not see us. As we watched from the doorway, he took the road which led to the pub.

'So that's who it was in there,' I said. 'I thought as much. Good thing we didn't go in.'

'Let's see what he's been up to,' said Kenneth. 'He's sure to be gone at least half an hour.'

'I'm not interested now I know it's Mr Ward. He's always digging,' I said. 'First the gladioli, then the chicken run and now this.'

'I know he's always digging,' said Kenneth. 'Come on! He wasn't carrying anything when he came out, so he can't have found the treasure.' I think my brother had convinced himself by this time that treasure had been hidden in the cottage. I was not equally convinced. I was two years older than Kenneth. Besides, I was very much afraid of Mr Ward. I thought he was slightly mad and I wanted nothing to do with him or his affairs.

'We've nothing to dig with,' I said feebly.

'Don't be daft! His spade and things will be in there, won't they?'

I had no more excuses to offer. We crossed the road and sneaked in at the open doorway. Like the rest of the cottages, this one had no front hall. We found ourselves in what had been the parlour before the hermit had turned it into a pigsty. The only light came in through the doorway, for the window was filthy with grime and covered in cobwebs. The whole place stank horribly and we were very careful not to go near the walls.

Somebody ('I bet it was Mr Ward,' said Kenneth) had dug a deep, wide hole in the boardless floor. It reminded me of a grave. A spade and a pickaxe were lying on the ground near it.

'Let's get out of here,' I said.

We talked about the cottage as we walked home.

'There couldn't be treasure in a place like that,' I said.

'If there is, I bet the hermit put a curse on it,' my brother said. 'What did you make of Mr Ward's hole?'

'It could had been a grave. You don't think he's murdered somebody, do you?'

'He looks like a murderer. I call him a very sinister sort of man. I tell you what! Why don't we keep an eye on Mr Ward? —tail him, you know, like they do in the Secret Service.'

'He'd find out and complain to Aunt Kirstie or perhaps even go for us. If he *is* a murderer, then he must be fleeing from justice and he would be capable of anything,' I protested.

'Well, let's not actually tail him, then, but just sort of keep an eye on him. It ought to be easy enough because I've thought how we could get into that cottage garden if we really wanted to.'

'How? We can't manage that ladder. Much too heavy and if we asked Our Sarah or some others to help us carry it, we'd have to let them into the garden, too. Besides, Our Ern would sneak.'

'My plan wouldn't need anybody except you and me and that iron bar in Uncle Arthur's toolshed.'

'What's the idea, then?'

'I'll show you on Monday. Some big boys at our London school did it to get into the recreation ground from the canal bank without having to go all the way round by the road.'

CHAPTER 3

The Sheepwash

I guessed what Kenneth meant to do, although I doubted whether even our combined strength could accomplish it.

'The boys you mean were bigger and tougher than us,' I said.

'Oh, we shall manage all right. It's only a question of leverage. Mr Crandon told us that with proper leverage you could turn the world upside down if only you could find somewhere else to stand while you were doing it.'

'You'd have to stand on the moon, I should think. That would be the nearest.' (This, of course, was many years before the miracle occurred and men actually did land on the moon.)

'Well, be that as it may (that's another of Mr Crandon's gags), you know what I mean, because at home we got through the gap ourselves one Saturday morning when the park-keeper wasn't about, so on Monday we'll try with Uncle Arthur's iron bar. Tomorrow I think we'll go down to the sheepwash and see if we can spot Old Sukie again,' said Kenneth.

'On a Sunday?'

'Oh, I see what you mean.' The fact that we knew perfectly well that the sheepwash was forbidden to us could be passed over on weekdays, but to sin on a Sunday was different. There was the never-to-be-forgotten occasion on which, surprisingly, Uncle Arthur had decided to take us for a walk on a Sunday morning and as we reached the outskirts of the town we found a paper-shop open. Uncle Arthur went in and bought a

Sunday paper and came out with some nut-milk chocolate for us. We ate it, of course, but, although it was an almost unheard-of luxury, I cannot say I enjoyed it very much.

'Do you think we'll go to hell for eating things bought on a Sunday?' Kenneth had enquired.

'We didn't do the actual buying ourselves,' I pointed out.

'When Aunt Lally was talking about boys scrumping pears and strawberries off those people opposite and sharing them out, on a promise not to tell, she said the receiver was worse than the thief.'

'Yes, but Uncle Arthur didn't *steal* the chocolate. He bought it fair and square with his own money. Besides, we couldn't *refuse* it. He would have been awfully offended. Nut-milk chocolate is about the most expensive sweet you can buy.'

'Perhaps we could make up for eating it. Put ourselves right some way.'

'Give most of our next brandy balls to Our Ern?' (That year we had only a halfpenny a week pocket-money.)

'No, that would be going too far. I'll tell you what we'll do. We'll each put one brandy ball down the well as a sacrifice. That ought to get us in the clear.'

'We'd only have three left.'

'Yes, well, let's just add a private bit when we say our prayers tonight. That ought to do. Even God couldn't *really* expect us not to eat the chocolate when Uncle Arthur had bought it for us.'

As it turned out, when Sunday came and went, our consciences were clear. We spent no money, having none left to spend, and we even allowed Aunt Lally to pressurise us into going to Sunday school. She was always suggesting it and our usual response was to make ourselves scarce as soon as we could.

On this particular Sunday, however, we were unlucky. The blow fell at the very beginning of the day. We had come downstairs at nine because Aunt Lally always allowed herself what she called 'a long lie-in' on Sunday mornings, and were about to go over to Aunt Kirstie's when grandfather, seated as usual in his big leather-covered armchair, said,

'You'll breakfast and dine with us today. Kirstie and Arthur have business up at the manor.'

We asked no questions. Grandfather, in addition to his patriarchal appearance and dignified bearing, was autocratic and short-tempered and, I think, not very fond of children, having had eight of his own.

Kenneth said (daringly, I thought),

'They generally leave us something on their bedside table. We go in to say good morning and there's chocolate cream or something.'

'It's here,' said grandfather, pointing to the sideboard with the silver-topped ebony stick he always had by him. 'You may have it after breakfast.'

After breakfast, which was bacon and eggs and fried bread, but not nearly such good fried bread as Aunt Kirstie's, we were told to go upstairs again and put on our best clothes.

'But we never change until after Sunday dinner,' I said, looking down at my print frock.

'Your grandfather likes to see you dressed up pretty on a Sunday,' said Aunt Lally, ushering us up the stairs as though she thought we would cut and run if she were not there to superintend us. 'He'll give you a button-hole to wear to Sunday school if you're good children.'

'But we don't *go* to Sunday school. It's a waste of time,' said Kenneth.

'That's wicked talk,' said Aunt Lally, shocked. 'Besides, your cousins are coming to call for you at a quarter to ten. They *always* go to Sunday school in the morning, yes, and to Mission Hall at night.'

The only cousins still young enough to go to Sunday school were Uncle George's children, Cissie and Dannie. We despised them, and they disliked us. However, it was of no use to argue. Along with them we had to go. I had tumbled down the day before and was not anxious to exhibit my scars in public, so the triumph of Cissie and Dannie was complete when, near the beginning of the proceedings, the Sunday school superintendent, a bearded man with a cast in one eye, pointed straight at me and said sternly,

'Stop talking, that little girl with the scrazed nose!' (I was *not* talking. It was Cissie.)

However, we were free at last, and just as we reached grandfather's front gate and were discussing what there was likely to be for Sunday dinner—'Chicken, I hope,' said Kenneth—we saw Aunt Kirstie and Uncle Arthur coming towards us down the hill. We rushed up to them.

'Thank you for the chocolate cream pigs,' I said. 'We've been to Sunday school. It was horrible. We knew much more about the Romans than the teacher who took our class. She was just plain ignorant. She only knew what was in the Bible.'

'That's no way to talk,' said Aunt Kirstie, who always paid lip-service, but no more, to religious observances. 'Sunday school is very nice and proper.'

'Can we have dinner with you instead of with Aunt Lally?' asked Kenneth.

'No, that you can't. Lally has killed and plucked a chicken specially. Besides, ours isn't even in the oven yet.'

'Aunt Lally said you went to the manor house. Did you really?'

'Your aunt don't tell lies,' said Aunt Kirstie. 'You'll maybe hear all about it later on.'

'Was it about Mr Ward?'

'Now why on earth should you ask me that?'

'Only because Lionel let out one day that Mr Ward was some kind of relation of his. He said he was a remittance man. What does that mean, Aunt Kirstie?'

'Only that he's kept by the family and doesn't have to work for his living.'

'Why doesn't he?'

'Because he was a gentleman born and has delicate health. And now you'd better run along, else Lally's dinner will spoil and I'll get the blame for keeping you talking.'

'You know what *I* think,' said Kenneth, when Sunday dinner was over and we had been settled on our own in the sitting-room with copies of an uplifting but dull periodical which Aunt Lally bought each Saturday when she went to the town for her shopping. '*I* think Mr Ward is an ex-convict and Mrs

Kempson or someone pays Aunt Kirstie to look after him, because the family don't want to own him any more. Lionel practically said as much, you know.'

'He could even be a lunatic,' I said. 'He acts like one at times.'

'We ought to be careful. He might be a *criminal* lunatic, and we did wonder whether he was a murderer. I'm glad we don't sleep at Aunt Kirstie's.'

'Why do you think they had to go to the manor house? It was *something* to do with Mr Ward. I'm sure of it.'

'Perhaps to ask for more money for looking after him.'

'Aunt Kirstie wouldn't do that.'

'Well, perhaps Uncle Arthur would.'

'I don't think they went of their own accord. I think they were sent for. It would be much more likely.'

'Oh, I don't know. They're not Mrs Kempson's servants.'

Speculation was idle. We gave it up, but, on the following day, when we were able to resume our normal routine, our suspicions that Mr Ward was not altogether *compos mentis* received a new fillip. We went along to the sheepwash in search of Our Sarah and her gang, for there was no sign of Lionel that morning and this was disappointing, since we had planned to ask him whether he knew of our relatives' visit to the manor house in the hope that he might be able to tell us something about it. However, nobody was at the sheepwash except Mr Ward. He stood up to his thighs in the water, swinging his pickaxe. Water and mud were flying in all directions and he himself was so wet that we could see the sun shining on the drops of water in his hair.

'Down!' whispered Kenneth.

'Where?'

'In the brook. He's got his back to us. Take your shoes off and leave them on the bank.'

'I've got stockings on.'

'They'll soon dry.' So we took off our shoes and waded into the brook where the bank was steepest and peered out at Mr Ward from behind the tall summer grasses. We gained nothing. Mr Ward hacked away with his pickaxe, sending up mud mixed with rainbow spray, then, suddenly, he lofted the pickaxe so that it described an arc before it fell fifteen feet away on to The Marsh. He took out his watch, looked at it, put it back in his pocket, came out of the sheepwash, regained his pickaxe and began to walk towards us.

We crouched down, my frock and Kenneth's shorts getting wetter and wetter, but apparently Mr Ward was unconscious of our presence. To our relief (although I now cannot see that we had anything to fear) he passed by us on the drove road and made his way back to the plank bridge. We gave him a good ten minutes, I should think, before we followed him on to grandfather's land and up to Aunt Kirstie's house for a washing-day dinner.

As usual, Mr Ward did not eat with us. He went up to his room by way of the back stairs, changed his wet clothes and went out again. We were anxious to follow him, but the food—cold roast pork and jacket potatoes—was already on the table, so we sat down quickly to conceal our wet clothes and began our meal.

We always hated washing-day. At home where the scullery in our London house was very small and most of the space was taken up by the copper, the gas-cooker and the sink, it was worse, but even at Aunt Kirstie's the whole of the downstairs smelt of heat and suds and wet clothes and our dinner was plonked down in front of us while Aunt Kirstie, with pink, horrid-looking, water-softened hands, flushed and perspiring brow, untidy hair and sleeves rolled up above her elbows, continued with her rinsing and wringing and Aunt Lally helped her by hanging out the clothes on a long line which stretched the whole length of the garden.

We ate our dinner as fast as we could. There were no 'afters' on washing-day unless there was some apple pie or baked rice or bread and butter pudding left over from Sunday, and on this particular Monday there was nothing, although Aunt Kirstie called out that we could have a bit of bread and jam if we liked.

Kenneth, however, was too anxious to put his plan into execution to stop for anything as unexciting as bread and jam, so we put our empty plates together, got the iron bar out of Uncle Arthur's shed the minute the garden was clear of Aunt Lally, and made for the iron fence at the bottom of the hermit's garden.

It was simple enough. Two of the iron uprights of the fence were soon forced apart by our united efforts with the bar and we were able to squeeze through the opening without much trouble, although it was fortunate that we were thin and had narrow heads. The garden was overgrown with tall, rank grass, thistles, docks, nettles and every other kind of weed. There were elder bushes, currant bushes long untended, some raspberry canes and near the back of the cottage a collection of empty tins which seemed to prove that the hermit had eaten other things besides Miss Summers' discarded loaves. At the bottom of the garden there was a doorless, stinking earth-closet and an equally doorless woodshed out of which a rat scurried at our cautious approach.

The back door had gone, as we knew. We stepped inside with caution, listening before we took each forward step, but it was evident the place was still empty. Moreover, again it smelt so fetid and unpleasant that there was no temptation to linger. A doorway separated the kitchen from the front room so, after peering through it at the scene of Mr Ward's labours and noting that his spade and pickaxe had gone, we retired to the back garden to think things over.

'Well I shan't be in a hurry to go in *there* again,' said Kenneth. 'I shouldn't be surprised if you couldn't catch all sorts of diseases in a place like that. You could even catch the plague, I shouldn't wonder. Rats carry it, you know.'

'Only overseas rats,' I said. 'Did you think Mr Ward had made his hole any bigger?'

'Quite a bit. Deeper, too, from what I could see of it.'

'What about the treasure?'

'He would have found it by now.'

'Unless it's hidden upstairs.'

'Dare you to go up!'

'No dare taken, so fainities.'

'That's for playing "he". It's no good for getting out of a dare.'

'Well, you've got to un-dare me, then.'

'All right. What shall we do now?'

'Make raspberry wine, if Aunt Kirstie will find us two bottles and some sugar.'

'She won't. Don't you remember last year when mine fermented in the night and blew its cork up to the ceiling and all the wine spilt over on to the dressing-table cover? Aunt Lally was furious, not about the dressing-table, but because the noise frightened her so.'

'I expect she thought it was a shot.'

'Oh, no, she must be used to hearing shots. Somebody is always going after rabbits on Lye Hill.'

'The gypsies, I suppose.'

'Shouldn't think so. They don't use guns, they use snares.'

'I wish we could go up Lye Hill. I don't believe the gypsies steal children and sell them as slaves. That's just a story to frighten us.'

'They might kidnap us and hold us to ransom, I suppose.'

'No, they wouldn't. Our relations haven't enough money. They might kidnap Lionel, though. Would you go up Lye Hill and rescue him if they did?'

'No. We'd only get into trouble for going up there when we've been told not to.'

'Well, we're not supposed to play down at the sheepwash, but we do. I vote we go to the sheepwash tomorrow. Mr Ward might be there again, doing his madman act with that pick-axe.'

'Better still, we might meet Old Sukie again. She's my friend. She gave me a paper flower. I want to ask her if she'll tell my fortune.'

'She's a witch, not a fortune-teller. Besides, before they'll tell your fortune you have to cross their palm with silver.'

'What does that mean?'

'I think it means you have to give them two bob. I believe it's the only coin which has a cross on it.'

'I tell you what. I expect she'll have a tent at the fair. It might be cheaper there.'

'But we aren't going to the fair. It's on the day we go home.'

'How do you know?'

'Our Sarah told me when it's held. All the village kids save up all the year for it and do jobs, and all that, to get money to spend. There are swings and roundabouts and coconut shies and hoop-la and shooting galleries and goodness knows what. How I jolly well wish we *could* go.'

'We wouldn't have much to spend if we *did* go, so perhaps it's just as well we can't.'

Our Sarah and the gang were down at the sheepwash. There was no sign of Mr Ward and Old Sukie did not come down Lye Hill.

CHAPTER 4

Tea-Party and After

We heard no more about the visit Aunt Kirstie and Uncle Arthur had paid to Hill House. We had remarked on the fact that, although Lionel Kempson-Conyers had been twice to tea with us, there had been no reciprocal invitation, yet when it came it found us unprepared and shy. For one thing, it was given in a note from his grandmother, Mrs Kempson herself, and not merely by word of mouth from Lionel. Moreover, it seemed to call for a written answer. Another problem was that of clothes. Lionel was always informally clad when he came down the hill to play with us, but Aunt Lally decided that we must wear our Sunday best if we were going to tea at the manor house.

'But we can't have any fun if Margaret wears her velvet frock and I have to put on a suit,' complained Kenneth. 'I shall ask Lionel what he thinks we ought to wear.'

'If his granny sends a proper invite,' said Aunt Lally, 'it means tea in the drawing-room, and tea in the drawing-room means Sunday clothes.'

'It won't be in the drawing-room,' I said. 'It will be in the nursery or the schoolroom. I've read about it in library books. Rich people's children never have tea in the drawing-room.'

Kenneth and I, who had heard from the village children all about the importance and glory of the manor house, decided that Mrs Kempson wanted to look us over to find out whether, in her opinion, we were suitable companions for her grandson.

However, the aunts in conclave decided that it was our grandfather's position as patriarch and part-owner of the village which was responsible for the honour accorded us, and that we must uphold the family dignity, so I wore my green velvet with the real lace collar and Kenneth his best suit and the bow tie he had for Christmas. We felt smart, uncomfortable and apprehensive. We had hoped Lionel would come for us, but we were left to make our own way. It seemed a long trek up the hill, yet, on the other hand, we seemed to get to the manor house long before we felt ready to face the ordeal before us.

I know now that it was a beautiful old house. At the time it merely intimidated me. A long gravel drive bordered by lime trees led up to it and our first problem was whether we ought to seek admittance by the imposing front door or go round to the back.

While we were hesitating, a young man drove up in what would nowadays be a vintage car, but which, at that time, I suppose, was one of the newest models. As he did so, the front door opened and a stately, bald-headed man-servant appeared.

'Oh, Barker, see that they put the car away, will you? I shan't be needing it again today,' said the young man. 'Hullo,' he said to us, 'are you the merchants who kicked off the cartshed roof and tried to drown yourselves in the sheepwash? Good! Come on in.' He led us past the stately butler and we found ourselves in what appeared to me to be a vast, baronial hall. It had a splendid staircase leading up from it and on the wall of the staircase were portraits. It was awe-inspiring and filled me with renewed apprehension.

The stately butler collected the young man's light overcoat and driving gloves and Kenneth's cap. I stood aside and furtively dusted the toes of my shoes against my stockings.

'All right, Barker, we'll show ourselves up,' said the young man. 'How *is* my mother?'

'You will find the mistress in her usual good health, sir.'

'The people from Paris arrived yet?'

'With Miss Amabel, yes, sir.'

'Good. Well, now, I'm Nigel Kempson. Who are you two?'

he said to us. 'I know you're Lionel's friends, but not your names.'

'Margaret and Kenneth Clifton,' I said. We mounted the splendid staircase and at the end of a short landing the young man flung open double doors painted in white and gold and having what I thought at the time were real gold handles, and said,

'What ho, everybody! Hullo, Lionel! I've brought along your companions in crime.'

It was an enormous room which dwarfed the people in it. I was too confused and shy at the moment to tell how many there were, but I know now that there were not more than seven or eight. Old Mrs Kempson was there, seated near an enormous Tudor fireplace in which a very small log fire was burning, and grouped around the room were a number of people of both sexes and of different ages among whom were Lionel's parents (we were told) and his sister. There were other introductions. Nobody shook hands, as we were accustomed to do at home when we met new people, but they nodded kindly and some of them smiled.

The point which immediately struck me was that Aunt Lally had been right about clothes. Lionel was wearing a smart black jacket and beautifully-creased light-grey trousers which made Kenneth's Sunday outfit look low-class and shoddy. He had come forward from his seat on a big leather *pouffe* as soon as we entered the room. He looked elegant and at ease and seemed like a stranger.

'Hullo,' he said. 'Glad you could come. Grandmamma, this is Margaret and this is Kenneth.'

Mrs Kempson, whom we had sometimes seen in the village, smiled rather frostily at us after Lionel had made the other introductions (with a *sang froid* which I envied him) and said, graciously *grande dame*:

'I hear you have been very kind to Lionel.' She then told us to sit on a sofa. A bit later on she said,

'Well, Lionel, you may run along now. You must bring your little friends back here when they are ready to go home at six and they will say goodbye to me.'

So it was schoolroom tea after all, or, rather, it was tea in the housekeeper's room. It was a very good tea, too. There was bloater paste as well as jam, chocolate biscuits and little buns as well as a big plum cake. The housekeeper was an intimidating, unsmiling, elderly little woman, but, having poured out tea and re-filled the pot, she left us to ourselves.

During the meal there was almost no conversation. After a preliminary period during which Kenneth and I ate in our most genteel way, stiffness and formality were abandoned and, without wasting time in talking, we stuffed ourselves with the riches of the loaded table. The housekeeper looked in once or twice, but she said nothing and went away again immediately.

'Well, that's that, then,' said Lionel when, regretfully, we had to admit that we could not manage to eat any more. 'There isn't time to do much, so would you rather come outside or go up and see my playroom?'

'What would we do outside?' asked my brother.

'Nothing, really. There's never anything to do here. We could skate stones on the pond, if you like.'

We opted for the playroom, hoping that he had some good toys and also mindful (at least, *I* was) that we were wearing our best clothes and that these and a pond might not harmonise. The playroom was at the very top of the house; in fact, it was one of the attics. Lionel's bedroom was next door and opened out of it.

He had not much in the way of toys, but there was a tin roundabout which worked when you wound it up, although the musical-box on it was broken. We played with this and with a few other things such as a humming-top and a small game of skittles. The roundabout, however, reminded me of St Swithin's Fair. I asked Lionel whether he would be going to it.

'When is it?'

'Saturday.'

'Then I won't be able to. It's my sister's birthday party. I don't suppose they'd let me go, anyway.'

'We shan't be going, either,' said Kenneth. 'We go home on

Saturday afternoon because our London school starts on Monday, worse luck.'

We had told lies to Our Sarah and the other children about the amount of money we would spend at the fair because we knew the truth would never come out. Of course we had nothing to spend, or so we thought.

'You're going home?' said Lionel. 'Oh, you can't do that! Who shall I have to play with? I'm stuck here for another three weeks.'

'There's your sister's birthday party,' said Kenneth.

'That's no good to me. She's inviting a lot of idiotic girls she used to be at school with, and their brothers, and Nigel's friends. It will be nothing but dancing and charades and all that sort of rot. In fact, I believe there's even some talk of fancy dress.'

'You'll look nice as Little Lord Fauntleroy,' said Kenneth unwisely. I separated them before any damage was done. At six o'clock we went home. Mrs Kempson said we must come again, but I did not think she meant it.

'I feel sorry for Lionel,' said Kenneth, as we walked down the drive and out past the lodge where nobody had lived since the old lodgekeeper died. 'It will be rotten for him when we've gone. Tell you what. Let's leave him the hermit's cottage.'

'Well, don't tell him yet. He blabs, you know, to that uncle. The uncle knew all about us, didn't he?'

'Well, we shan't need the cottage any more after Saturday. When we see him next time, let's swear him to keep it a secret and take him there. After all, that was a jolly decent tea he gave us, better than ours to him.'

'Oh, I don't know. I don't suppose he has kippers for tea up at the house. I believe rich people only eat them for breakfast and rich children wouldn't have them even then, I don't suppose. They only get porridge, I think.'

'Well, we've got to leave the cottage to *someone*. Even Our Sarah and Our Ern don't go there any more, so they don't know how exciting it's become. Besides, they wouldn't think as much of that grave as Lionel would.'

'All right, then,' I said doubtfully, 'but I expect he'll get into an awful row if he gets his clothes mucked up or takes back fleas or bugs or anything, and then he'd be sure to split and say we took him there.'

'*We* have never taken home bugs.'

'Only because we're careful never to go near the walls.'

'We could warn him.'

'All right, then, we'll tell him all about it, but only just before we go home.'

My father was to have come down on Saturday morning to take us back, but there was a surprise because we did not go. It turned out that my mother had had a fall and was in hospital, so on the Thursday there came a letter to ask whether we could stay on for a bit, as my father could not stay away from work to look after us and our little brother Bruce. A neighbour would take on Bruce, but no arrangements could be made about us because no one wanted to look after school-age children, even well-behaved ones.

I suppose we were sorry that mother had to go to hospital, but my first emotion, I am ashamed to say, was one of elation to think that we would be staying on in the village and might even be able to persuade Uncle Arthur to take us to the fair on Saturday after all.

'We still haven't got any money, though,' Kenneth said sadly, 'and a fair isn't any fun at all without money.' It turned out, however, that father had enclosed a postal order with his letter. It was for the princely sum of five shillings (old money) and to us it seemed a fortune. 'There are plenty of things you can have a ride on for twopence,' said Kenneth, 'and Our Ern told me about "a penn'orth on the mat" and that there are two roundabouts, one a penny a go and a little one, with only horses, not cocks and ostriches and things, for only a ha'penny.'

The next thing was to get Uncle Arthur to take us. This he proved willing to do.

'I used to be a devil among the coconuts,' he said, 'and I once got a prize at the shooting gallery. Remember when I laid four coconuts and a china doll in your lap, Kirstie?'

'I remember when you went into that wrestling booth to

win five pounds and nearly got your neck broken,' said Aunt Kirstie. 'You were a fool in those days, Arthur.'

'Ah. Pity it wasn't boxing. I'd have won at that,' said Uncle Arthur, not at all put out by her candid criticism.

'What did you make of Lionel's people?' I asked. It was the morning of the fair, the day we had expected to be going home, so we had to discuss mundane matters in order to cope with our inward excitement. It was like Christmas Eve, but even more so, because we had never been to a fair before.

'Well, we didn't see much of them. I suppose they were all right,' said Kenneth. 'I didn't think much of Lionel's toys. Ours are better.'

'I expect he has others at home. His mother looked rather stuck up. Perhaps she thought we weren't good enough for Lionel. I didn't care for his sister much, either.'

'Was she the one who giggled with the uncle or whatever he is, and didn't take any notice of us? Lionel doesn't like her. He says he wishes she was a brother and would take him fishing. I wonder what her birthday party will be like?'

'Lionel told us. Dancing, and all that, and perhaps fancy dress. Do you really think he'll have to dress up? I bet they'll have jolly good things to eat, anyway,' I said enviously.

'That was a very decent tea that old woman gave us. She looked a bit strict, though. And the servant who took my cap! He picked hold of it as though I'd got nits in my hair.'

'Wonder what Lionel's doing this morning?'

'I expect,' said Kenneth, giggling, 'he's having a special bath and his hair shampooed, ready for the party tonight. Let's go down to the sheepwash and see if Mr Ward's there again. He's a lunatic, must be.'

'We'll have to make sure he doesn't spot us. He's a *dangerous* lunatic, I'm sure,' I said earnestly.

'Oh, well, it's not as though he knows we know he digs in the hermit's cottage,' said Kenneth. 'We'll have to keep mum about that.'

Down by the brook we found Our Sarah with Our Ern and the rest of the hangers-on. This was surprising, for in Our

Sarah's cottage, we knew, Saturday was bedroom day and she was usually kept at home to help turn out the rooms, change the sheets and clean the floors. Bedroom day was an institution among poor families in my childhood, but in London it was usually celebrated on Fridays and the bigger girls were kept away from school regularly on Friday in term-time so that they could help with the chores. In Our Sarah's home, however, bedroom day was on Saturday and she carried out the whole operation on her own, while her mother shopped at the Co-op and her father spent money at the pub.

'Hoy, you young Oi say,' she called out as we approached. 'Where be you a-goen?'

'To the sheepwash,' Kenneth replied.

'You don't warnt to be a-goen there today. You stop along of us and see the band and the percession,' said Our Sarah authoritatively.

'What band?'

'This be 'Orspital Sat'day. They always has it on Saint Swithin's.'

'Are you playing hookey?' asked Kenneth, always bolder at putting direct questions than I was.

'How jer mean?'

'I thought your mother made you work on Saturdays.'

'Us be letten the bedrooms go for thes once. Me dad's en the band.'

'Oh, isn't it the Salvation Army band?'

'No, t'ent, then. 'Tes the town band. They always leads the percession on 'Orspital Sat'day. They haves people dressed up and en masks and they haves boxes what they comes up and rattles at ee, and you puts en an a'penny ef you got one. You got an a'penny, you young Oi say?'

'Yes, but I want it for the fair,' said Kenneth. 'Besides, collections are for grown-ups. They won't expect children to pay.'

So we perched ourselves on the coping of the little bridge which carried the culvert and prepared to watch the procession go by.

'Where ded you get to Wednesday?' asked Our Ern.

'Tea at the manor house.'

'Garn! You never!'

'All right, then. Ask Lionel.'

'What you have for tea?'

'Ordinary bread and butter, currant bread and butter, bloater paste, jam, chocolate biscuits, little jammy buns, plum cake and cups of tea.'

'Garn! Bet ee daren't walk under the bredge,' said Ern, changing the subject. (The culvert under the bridge was no higher than a big drain.)

'I will, if you will,' said Kenneth.

'Garn! Oi done et before. Oi done et a dozen toimes.'

'Oh, yes? You and who else?'

At this moment we heard the sound of the approaching band and I hoped this would deter Kenneth, but it did not. He slid down the bank and waded into the brook. I went to the end of the bridge where he would emerge and waited anxiously. It did not take him long, but I thought he looked very pale when he climbed out and his shorts were soaked to the top of his thighs.

'There you are, then,' he said, walking up to Ern. 'And now you can have this.' With this remark he uppercut Ern and knocked him backwards into the brook. I prepared to take Kenneth's side if Our Sarah decided to intervene, but when Ern crawled out and began to blubber, all she said was:

'Serve ee glad for tellen loies. You never walked under there in your loife. He be twoice the man what you be. Hold yer howlen. Here 'em comes.'

We did not know Sarah's father, so could not pick him out from among the other bandsmen, but we yelled and clapped and Sarah and Ern (who was wet and muddy, but had taken his sister's advice and stopped howling) fell in behind the band, which already had a following of children.

'Come on,' said Kenneth; but I hung back and even retreated on to The Marsh. Not many things frightened me, but people wearing masks always did and still do. There was not much in the way of a procession except for a set of Morris dancers whose caperings did not fit in with the tune the band was playing. There were, however, a dozen or more creatures in the most terrifying get-up I had ever seen except in pictures. They were prehistoric animals, dinosaurs, I suppose, and they looked like demented crocodiles or the sort of giant lizards you might see in a nightmare.

Attached to their claws were collecting-boxes made of tin which they rattled as they pranced along behind the Morris dancers and the band. Although they were nightmarish, they were horribly realistic, too; nothing like the things which can be made nowadays for such films as the *Argonauts* and *Sinbad the Sailor*, of course, but dreadfully frightening, all the same. When they came up close and shook their collecting boxes, some people, I am sure, hastily dropped coppers into the rattling tins just to get rid of them.

Personally, I let them go by before I followed on and then I walked very slowly, so that by the time I reached Aunt Kirstie's gate the band, the dancers and the masked importunists were away up the hill and the music was almost inaudible.

'They're going up to the manor house,' said Kenneth, 'but Aunt Kirstie says they may be coming back this way. The collectors are medical students. Aren't they grand? They're prehistoric animals, you know. I wish I had a costume like that. Why didn't you come along? One of them picked me up and pretended to bite my head off. It was grand. Some of the women screamed. It was terrific.'

'I want my dinner,' I said, 'so I shan't bother to go to the front gate if they do come back this way.' Nothing, I felt, would induce me to encounter those fearsome beings again, and that was before we heard about the murder.

CHAPTER 5

Mrs Kempson Puts Pen to Paper

I am sure of my facts, dear Mrs Bradley. I can assure you of that. I have kept a journal ever since the death of my husband and it is to that which I have referred in beginning this statement to you. The particulars are as concise but, I hope, as complete as it is possible for me to make them. I realise that you have many commitments, but I shall be immensely relieved when you are free to take my brother as your patient. His conduct has become most disquieting and I am in urgent need of professional assistance in determining what is best to be done, both in his interests and my own.

The death of my husband did not, in itself, sadden me. His last illness was prolonged and very distressing, and the termination of his life some ten years ago was a blessed relief to both of us. It was then, as I say, that I took to keeping a journal. It filled a gap and helped to pass a somewhat lonely existence. My only child, a girl, is married and lives mostly abroad, as her husband is attached to one of our embassies. She has two children, Amabel (now at finishing school in Paris) and a young son Lionel, still at his preparatory school.

Sometimes the children come to me for a week or two during the summer, but otherwise my life is lonely and not very interesting, as my only other close relation is my brother Ward, the subject of this analysis. I should add that I have an adopted son, Nigel, but the adoption is not a legal one and there is no question of Nigel's having any claim on me or on the estate. He is supposed to be the son (illegitimate, I fancy) of an actor-manager for whom my late husband, a very wealthy man (fortunately for me!), once acted as an angel—for so, I believe, they call the backers of theatrical enterprises. Nigel's mother, I feel sure, was the leading lady in the production financed by my husband. It sometimes crosses my mind that Nigel may even be the illegitimate son of my husband himself and this actress, as so much was done in putting him to public school and university and then finding him a well-paid sinecure of a job in London with a firm in which my husband had a controlling interest. My husband, in fact, sometimes urged that we should take out adoption papers, but this was a course I steadfastly opposed, as I felt that it was against my daughter's interests.

However, Nigel has always treated Hill House as his home and has proved himself the dearest and most considerate of boys. Nevertheless, I cannot sufficiently stress that there is no consanguinity between us and that he has no claim on anything but my sincere affection. Unfortunately, since he left College and took a flat in London to be near his work, I have seen all too little of him. We meet almost as strangers until the ice is broken by our very real affection for one another, but, even so, his visits come all too seldom.

In view of what I have to tell you, it is necessary to stress the fact that not only has Nigel no claim upon me, but that he has known, ever since he left College, that he has few expectations from me. He has accepted this. He knows that the estate must go to little Lionel and that a great deal of money is needed to keep it up.

Apart from my husband's last illness, I have had only one major anxiety in my life and that, as you will have guessed, is the conduct of my brother Ward. He was always an ill-behaved, malicious child and his way of life did not improve as he grew older. After he had been expelled from two schools the only institution which would accept him as a pupil was a seminary run by the Jesuits. From this he absconded and the next we heard of him was from Canada.

Years passed and my father died. This meant that, as this

estate is entailed in the male line, Ward was entitled to inherit. The lawyers made efforts to trace him, but without success. More time went by and then a letter came from New York State to say that Ward had spent fifteen years in an American prison, was released, but destitute, and wanted his fare paid so that he could come home. He promised to behave himself if my parents would have him back. Of course, by that time both were dead and my husband, too. I was living here in my old home and the very last thing I wanted was to have Ward on my hands, so I did not answer the letter. This was several years ago.

The next thing was another letter, this from an unknown woman in New York, to say that she had heard from a reliable source that my wretched brother was dead. She said that she had been living with him and keeping him before he quarrelled with her and left her, but she had found my address among some effects he had left behind him when they parted. In view of this, I saw no reason for not staying on in this house, which, after all, was my girlhood home, looking after the place and acting (since his parents were abroad) as caretaker for little Lionel who, so far as I knew, would inherit as soon as he came of age. The woman made no mention in her letter of marriage or of children, so, naturally, I assumed that, with Ward dead, Lionel would be the heir.

Imagine my horror, therefore, dear Mrs Bradley, when, a year later, I received a visit from an individual who claimed to be my brother. I was writing a letter to my daughter at the time, I remember, when Barker announced that a person named Ward had called and was asking to see me.

'Ward?' I said 'Surely not!'

'That, madam, is the name the individual gave.'

'What kind of person is he?'

'I could not take it upon myself to say, madam.'

I knew, by this answer, that, in Barker's opinion, the caller was not what he would have described as a gentleman and yet was someone of indeterminate status who might, after all, warrant being shown into my presence.

'Very well,' I said. 'I will see him.'

'In here, madam?'

'No. Show him into the library.' I finished my letter before I went down and then I made as impressive an entrance as I could. A middle-aged man in a suit which was obviously ready-made came towards me with the intention, it seemed, of embracing me. I noticed that he was wearing gloves, I suppose to hide his prison-calloused hands, and was also wearing pince-nez.

'Good afternoon,' I said, in my most formal tones. 'You wish to speak to me? Are you one of the tenants?' (I knew, of course, that he was not.)

'I'm the one and only tenant, my dear sister,' he replied. 'I'm your brother. The black sheep returns to the fold.'

'I have no brother,' I said. 'My only brother died in New York more than a year ago.'

'I can produce proofs of my identity, you know,' he said, 'proofs which I think a lawyer would accept, even if you will not.' He smirked and brushed his untidy moustache.

'Produce them, then,' I said. 'Meanwhile, perhaps you will be good enough to leave my house.'

'*Your* house?' he said. I rang for Barker to show him out. He went without any fuss and the next thing was a letter from our family lawyers. A man had been to see them claiming that he was my brother and heir to the estate.

'As you will know,' the letter said, 'the estate was entailed several generations ago and the entail has never been revoked. The man we interviewed has produced certain proofs of identity which could form the basis of long and expensive litigation should you decide to contest his claim in favour of your grandson, the apparent heir to the estate. We are of the opinion that in all likelihood the man is an impudent impostor, but proving this might be a matter of extreme difficulty in view of the papers in his possession and what appears to be his extensive knowledge of the family history. We await your further instructions.'

I was in a quandary, so I wrote back to the lawyers and asked their advice, but they merely reiterated that, in their opinion, I might find litigation both lengthy and expensive, with no certainty at the end that I should win my case. Then Ward came to see me again. I told him that he could not prove he was my brother. He replied that I would have infinite trouble proving that he was not.

'Look,' he said, 'I have reformed, I can assure you of that. I shan't be any trouble to you. All I want is an allowance and a home. I need not live here. You would not want that. If you will find me somewhere respectable and quiet and give me ten pounds a week, I'll trouble you no further and I won't even visit you any more. Come, Emilia, what do you say?'

'If you really are my brother, go ahead and claim your inheritance,' I said.

'Oh, the estate brings in little or nothing. I know that,' he said. 'Even if I had it, I could not afford to keep up the house and pay the servants. Why not make the best of a bad job and do as I suggest? It will save both of us trouble and you a great deal of money. You don't really want to go to law, you know.'

'What makes you think I can afford to pay you ten pounds a week?' I asked.

'Oh, I know our parents left very little, but you must be very well off since your husband died,' he answered.

'Be that as it may,' I said, 'it can hardly concern anybody but my heirs, and you can hardly expect to be one of those.'

'Oh, I don't, I don't, my dear sister,' he declared. 'I know that you have an adopted son. I suppose he will be the chief beneficiary.'

'You seem to have interested yourself vastly in my affairs,' I said angrily. 'However, since it seems just as well to clear the matter up between us once and for all, I may as well tell you that my adopted son, as you call him, has no claim on me whatever and he knows it. I do not say I shall leave him nothing. I am very fond of him. However, it will not and cannot be anything at all substantial because I have a duty to others bound to me by ties of blood; others whom my dear husband made me promise, before he died, that I would benefit.' (This, I confess, Mrs Bradley, was not quite true!) I went on:

'You rightly point out that most of what I have was left to

me by him and my conscience would not permit me to dispose of it against his wishes. He was particularly anxious that not more than five thousand should go to Nigel. The boy is not of our kin and we have done much to further his interests, first my husband and now myself. The bulk of the money will go to my grandson.'

'And I am to get nothing? Oh, well, I did not expect very much. You could spare me fifty a month and not miss it, though, couldn't you, dear sister, if only for old times' sake?' he suggested.

'I have no pleasant memories of old times, so far as you are concerned,' I said.

'Will you do nothing for me? After all, I am prepared to give up all claim to the estate. That ought to be worth a modest thirty thousand pounds at your death. I should not expect to claim it before that.'

'Thirty thousand pounds?'

'Left to me in your will.' He paused and then said, astonishingly, 'You can add a clause specifying that I get it provided you die a natural death, of course.'

'I will talk it over with Nigel,' I said feebly. 'Meanwhile I will pay you five pounds a week and will make myself responsible for your board and lodging, but only on condition that you sign an undertaking not to molest me and not to make any further demands upon my purse.'

'Except for the thirty thousand, dear sister. That is my condition and the only one on which I shall accept your terms. Otherwise I'm out to make trouble,' he said. 'The estate is mine, and you know it. I could turn you out of this house tomorrow if I chose, and as for your dependents, whoever they are—you have children and grandchildren, I dare say—well, they can go hang, so far as I'm concerned. If you won't meet my terms, I'll damn well get a son of my own—I'm not past doing that, you know—so I advise you to think it over.'

Well, dear Mrs Bradley, I agreed to his terms, whether wisely or not I hardly know. The thirty thousand will still leave plenty for little Lionel and I am leaving only five thousand to Nigel, as he knows. My lawyers are not very happy about the arrangements, but since Ward is prepared to give up all claim to the estate I feel that he is entitled to some benefit. He now lodges with a most respectable couple in the village here. The wife's father is a substantial man and the couple have a very good house for such people. They let Ward have two upstairs rooms and his food, for all of which I pay, and until recently I had had no complaints from them about his behaviour.

To make certain that the Landgraves received their money I should much have preferred that Nigel should ride down the hill and deliver it to them personally in a sealed envelope containing coin of the realm, but Nigel lives in London, so now one of the servants takes it. The rest of the allowance, the five pounds a week remittance, I send Ward monthly in the form of money orders which he cashes at the village post-office and spends mostly, I believe, at the public house.

The first inkling I had that matters are no longer quite what they ought to be came in the form of a letter from Mrs Landgrave. It was very well put together, but I believe her education was superior to that of her husband, although I believe him to be a good sort of man in his way, sober and respectable, I mean. Well, in the letter Mrs Landgrave informed me that, while she had no wish to complain, they had become worried about certain changes in the conduct of 'Mr' Ward.

'He has always liked digging,' she wrote. 'At first he dug in the bit of our garden we let him have, but now he has dug up and destroyed all my husband's gladdies.' (Gladioli I suppose she meant.) 'Then he got into my father's chicken run,' she went on, 'and began to dig there. He said he was digging for buried treasure, which did not seem to us very likely. His latest has been to go digging on The Marsh and I think he must have been in the sheepwash, for he came back wet through, right to his hair, and plastered in mud, so we would be much obliged if you would see into things, as it does not seem very sensible behaviour, but more like a child or somebody not quite right in the head. I should tell you that he has also bought himself a pickaxe, which I don't see he can find any proper use for, as well as a new and heavy spade to dig with.'

When the groom took the next week's rent for Ward's rooms and food, I enclosed a note to ask the woman and her husband to come up and see me, for Mrs Landgrave's letter convinced me that they had reason for complaint. Nobody wants to give house-room to a madman.

Apart from that, the news disquieted me for two other reasons. As a young man, my brother had been in trouble for trying to dig up corpses in a churchyard. He said he wanted to raise the devil and that a corpse was needed for this. The other point was that the Landgraves' story has helped to convince me that Ward really *is* my brother and, as such, has a right to more than his board, lodging and pocket-money, as Nigel and I agreed. It is true that the estate eats up more than it brings in, nevertheless, although the heir cannot sell or otherwise dispose of it, there is nothing to prevent him from developing the place, say, as a guest-house or private hotel.

The grounds, too—they are extensive and the soil is fertile—could be developed agriculturally and made to pay, and there is a large covered market in the nearby town which I am sure could and would take the produce.

However, if Ward has become mentally unstable, as the Landgraves' evidence, given factually and without any show of indignation which, under the circumstances, I could scarcely have quibbled at, most definitely suggests, any attempt on his part at running the estate as a business proposition would be out of the question.

Another complication mentioned by Mrs Landgrave is that she has two young children staying next door with the grandfather and a widowed sister and taking all their meals with the Landgraves. This brings them into daily contact with Ward, so the Landgraves feel a natural anxiety on their account if Ward is becoming what they termed at our interview as 'peculiar'. Incidentally, as Lionel has struck up an acquaintance with these children, I am anxious on his behalf also. I have met the little pair and they seem well-mannered and intelligent and speak better than the village children do. I would not wish (apart from offending the Landgraves, on whose goodwill I am dependent) to forbid Lionel to go down to the village, but if Ward's mind is defective I wonder how safe my little grandson will be if Ward discovers (as well he may, for you know how children chatter) that he is Ward's dispossessor.

Ward has said that he does not want the property, but that was five years ago when I am sure that he was of sound mind. In view of what the Landgraves have told me, I am not able to adhere to that conviction. I am writing to say that I think the first step is for him to see a reputable psychiatrist. I shall be glad and relieved to welcome you to Hill House, therefore, at your very earliest convenience. I trust that, from what I have told you in this letter, you will appreciate that it will not be possible—practicable, perhaps I should say—to bring the patient to your London clinic.

You may still wonder why I gave in to Ward's demands. Of course I would have fought him on the occasion of his first visit to myself and my lawyers, in spite of advice that the odds were against me, for I am not the person to give in at all easily, but the fact is that there was something about his voice and manner—although not in his appearance—which made me almost certain that he was speaking the truth in claiming to be my brother. There was only a faint doubt in my mind. Something in me reached out to something in him, some fugitive memory, I suppose, of our childhood together, although I cannot remember ever really liking him.

I have, as I say, given in about the thirty thousand to be paid him at my death. I still feel that he ought to be compensated for giving up the estate and even with that substantial bite out of my fortune there will still be plenty left, as I say, for little Lionel. However, I have no intention of leaving thirty thousand pounds to a madman. I have discussed matters with Nigel by letter and he fully agrees with me that we should send for a psychiatrist, so do please come soon.

CHAPTER 6

All the Fun of the Fair

The fair had its roots in the dim and distant Middle Ages, but the only remaining vestiges of its original function, which was annual trading in goods brought by merchants from miles around and even from foreign parts, were the small booths and stalls on the outskirts of the space occupied by roundabouts and swings and all the other exciting and noisy pleasures on which most of the people (and especially the children) had come to spend their money.

Kenneth and I were in a fever all day. We had hoped to set off immediately after breakfast and spend the whole day at the fair, but Uncle Arthur thought otherwise. After tea was the time to go, he said, so Aunt Kirstie made us rest after the mid-day dinner and when, at last, we were ready to set off, she made us wear our overcoats and told Uncle Arthur on no account to keep us out late.

It was a long way to the bus stop and a long way from the bus terminus to the fair, or so it seemed to me at the age of ten. However, we could hear the raucous music as soon as we turned into Broad Street and I know our steps quickened at the sound of it.

St Swithin's Fair had nothing to do with St Swithin's legendary rain-making. It was so called because it was held in St Swithin's market-place, a large open square behind the covered market where we were taken for an occasional treat to eat lardy-cakes and look at the puppies, kittens, cage-birds,

Angora rabbits, Belgian hares and Flemish giants in the pet-shop. I can still remember the mingled odours and scents of the covered market—the sour smells of small animals, the heavenly smells of baking, flowers and fruit, the sweaty smell of people and the moist, earthy smell of freshly-watered ferns and plants in pots.

The fair was entirely different from the covered market. It was far more exciting. At any rate, it wildly excited Kenneth and me. We had expected much, but I am bound to say that St Swithin's Fair was no disappointment. Looking back now, after all these years, I realise that few things to which young children (after all, I was only ten years old and Kenneth eight) look forward, do turn out to be disappointing. Youthful imagination coupled with a desperate desire for wish-fulfilment sees to that, and therefore St Swithin's Fair stands out in my mind as one of the high spots in a moderately happy life. We did not need to seek for any kind of compensation. We thoroughly enjoyed ourselves.

For one thing, Uncle Arthur was to our minds an ideal companion, an easy-going, simple-minded, very indulgent sort of man. He was not native to the village, but came of Cockney ancestors. His mother was a virago who was accustomed literally to throw her husband and sons into the street when they came home drunk, and she had bestowed her thews and sinews and her generous, single-minded outlook, but not her flaming temper, upon Uncle Arthur. He had boxed in the East End for small purses, so was technically a professional, but he was a kindly man who lacked the killer instinct which brings a boxer fame and the big money.

At the fair he soon gave a taste of his muscular quality. He banged with a mallet on a sort of anvil and a weight shot up and rang a bell. He was given a cigar for that. Then he smashed a coconut and was given a whole one in exchange. We were thrilled and delighted, so much so that 'a penn'orth on the mat,' which he urged us to try, made me forget my fears of this sort of feat. I cascaded round the bends with some enjoyment and returned slightly dizzy but undoubtedly triumphant to Kenneth and Uncle Arthur after I and my mat had been fielded by a sweating man in a dirty singlet who stood at the foot of the tower.

After all these years, some of my impressions of the fair are rather blurred, like the reflections of brilliant lights on wet pavements while the rain is still pouring down. I remember that, although it was not yet dark when we arrived, the naked naphtha flares which lit up the scene were already hissing and windblown. I remember the jostling, shoving, good-humoured crowds, the gaily-painted swing-boats, and the raucous, heady, intoxicating music blaring from the roundabouts.

I remember that I nearly (but not quite) ringed a most desirable box of chocolates at the hoop-la stall and that Kenneth tried his luck with an airgun but failed to hit one of the ping-pong balls which were dancing up and down on jets of water, and I remember arguing with him as to whether or not you got a longer ride on the roundabout by taking one of the outside horses rather than one nearer the centre where the machinery and the music were.

'It stands to reason,' he said. 'It's a case of concentric circles. The outside one has the longest perimeter.'

'But it travels slower,' I said, 'so the actual length of the ride is the same.'

We tried a swing-boat with Uncle Arthur at one end and the two of us at the other. I did not like this very much because, as the boat swung higher, it seemed quite possible that at a certain point we could go clean over the top and loop the loop, so I was relieved when our time was up and the man in charge grounded us with a long wooden plank which jarred the boat uncomfortably and alarmingly but soon brought us to a standstill.

Uncle Arthur bought us bullseyes, brandy snaps and lardy-cakes and we drank so-called lemonade. Later on we had sausage rolls and ice-cream. (Ice-cream was a rare treat in those days and we seldom bought it for ourselves because it disappeared so quickly.) Soon after this, a clock on St Swithin's church struck ten and Uncle Arthur decided that it was time to think about going home.

We pleaded that there were several alleyways among the stalls which, so far, we had not explored and Kenneth (always much more generous and thoughtful than myself) said that he wanted to buy a present for Aunt Kirstie but had not seen anything he fancied she would like.

In one of the quieter by-ways there were stalls selling fancy goods such as sachets of lavender, garish pincushions covered in bead-work, boxes ornamented with sea-shells, fancy handkerchiefs and brightly-coloured hair-ribbons. The prices seemed high, so Kenneth and I (rather grudgingly on my part, I must admit) went shares in a pale-blue handkerchief which had a knot of pink flowers in one corner surrounding the letter K. Uncle Arthur put it in his pocket so that we should not lose it and a moment or so later we found ourselves on the edge of the fairground opposite a large marquee.

Behind it a narrow thoroughfare had been left so that traffic could still flow. On the other side of the thoroughfare was a pavement for foot-passengers and abutting on to this stood one of the several pubs which supplied the farmers and their men with food and beer on market days.

Outside the marquee a large board lit by two swinging lanterns on iron uprights advertised that there was a prize of five pounds for anyone who could wrestle successfully for five minutes against Tiger-Cat Bellamy Smith using catch-as-catch-can, Cornish style, Westmorland style, Japanese or lumberjack style, no holds barred, admission sixpence. Exhibition bouts would take place between challengers' efforts, it stated. It concluded, *Roll up, roll up! All the fun of the fair.*

Beside the board, vociferating at the top of his lungs, stood a fat man in a tight-fitting evening suit which had seen better days. For the benefit, apparently of those who could not read, he was declaiming the information printed on the board and emphasising the importance of the prize.

As we paused to watch and listen, a group of young men, noisy and somewhat drunk, came out of the public house and, after some bucolic argument punctuated by laughter and a few slurred oaths, they paid their sixpences and entered the marquee.

'Well now,' said Uncle Arthur, 'time we looked for that bus.' But he seemed in no hurry to move on, and while we waited and Kenneth squeezed my arm hopefully, several other customers went in to see the show. The busker outside redoubled his efforts and added to his repertoire.

'Roll up! Roll up! Only a few seats left. Roll up! Here's your chance! Five lovely thick uns to the winner. Roll up, gen'lemen sportsmen.' Then his eye picked us out although we stood in the gloom. 'Ladies and children half price,' he bellowed. 'Don't miss an educational treat! See the greatest wrestler on earth! Try your luck for five beautiful nicker! Come on! Roll up! Roll up! Next exhibition bout in a coupla minutes from NOW.'

Two or three more men went in. I could tell that Kenneth was in agony lest all the seats should be gone before Uncle Arthur had made up his obviously vacillating mind.

'Couldn't we just pop in, Uncle?' he said at last. 'It's only threepence for children and I've got that left. *Couldn't* we?'

'Oh, it's not for children,' said Uncle Arthur, but he still lingered.

'The man said it was educational, and it's only wrestling. It's not as though they're going to knock each other out,' I said.

'Wrestling's worse nor boxing,' said Uncle Arthur. 'Oh, well, all right, just for a few minutes, then.' Kenneth darted for the tent-flap, his threepence already in his hand, and Uncle Arthur and I followed. The marquee was full of noise, tobacco smoke and the smell of sweaty, beery men. There were still a number of unoccupied backless wooden benches. We sat down, Kenneth in the gangway seat, myself next to him and Uncle Arthur between me and a sleazy drunk who was singing sadly to himself and hiccupping now and then.

Instead of the usual ring, there was a stage, a small, square platform covered with coarse green matting. Some wooden steps led up to this from the auditorium. The fat man mounted these and announced in a voice gone husky from his previous open-air efforts:

'Presentin' a three-round, catch-as-catch-can exhibition contest between, on my right, Jacques Collins, on my left, Tiger-Cat Bellamy Smith. Gen'lemen will kindly stop smokin' while this important exhibition bout is in progress.'

No notice whatever was taken of this suggestion. He retired and the two wrestlers rose from the knees of their seconds, who had been kneeling on one knee and accommodating their principals on the other thigh.

The Tiger-Cat was lean and had black hair, long legs and thin, muscular arms. He was dressed in a black, long-sleeved vest and black tights. His opponent was shorter and more thick-set, with a bulging bull-neck and an eyebrow-length fringe of red hair. He wore sky-blue breeches which fastened under the knee; his chest, except for a menacing tangle of red hair, was bare to the waist. The two men advanced to the centre of the stage and danced about in a manner which was obviously only for show and hardly looked like business. Some of the audience lit such clay pipes as had gone out or any noisome cigars they had won at the fair. Others got out cheap cigarettes abstracted from battered packets, and we all settled down to enjoy the fun.

There was one more announcement before the exhibition bout really got under way.

'You are advised, gen'lemen sportsmen,' bellowed the fat man, advancing to the top of the steps again, 'to study the contest closely so as to pick up pointers as to FORM. The gen'lemen sportsmen contestants for our prize-money of five pounds will be matched against the loser of this exhibition contest. The *loser*, not the winner, gen'lemen sportsmen. Thank you.'

He then retreated to the centre of the stage and the contestants went back to their corners, but not to the knees of their seconds, for these had retired. Somebody rang a bell, the fat man (who was going to referee the bout) skipped out of the way and the wrestlers, bending forward from the waist, held their hands and arms at the ready as they began to circle round one another, looking for a hold.

The contest enthralled me, although Uncle Arthur muttered that it was rigged and that the winner knew he was booked to win and the loser knew he was to lose, and both knew exactly when the *dénouement* would come and the lambs (if any) among the audience be enticed to the slaughter. 'For there won't be no five-pound given, you can bet your bottom dollar,' said our cynical but knowledgeable uncle.

The contestants circled, feinted, rolled together on the matting, grunted, clutched and appeared to do everything short of strangling one another. The audience shouted and stamped and the affair went three rounds, but even by the end of the second round the thin fellow appeared to be getting the worst of it. At the beginning of the fourth round it was all over, and in the most sensational manner. The bulkier man suddenly, thrillingly and theatrically caught up his opponent bodily and literally flung him into the auditorium, where, true to his tiger-cat title, he landed miraculously on his feet in the clear space between the front of the stage and the first row of the backless benches. He climbed back on to the stage, shook his head as his opponent came forward and slouched off into the wings.

The victor bowed to the sporadic applause and the fat impresario came to the front of the stage again.

'See 'ow easy, gen'lemen sportsmen! Who's for winnin' five pounds? Don't all roll up at once. Come on, now. Who's goin' to try his luck? We'll just give the Cat time to get his breath back, and then....' Before he had time to finish, a thickset young countryman, propelled by the willing hands of his friends, was thrust, stumbling and protesting, to the foot of the wooden steps. The fat man stretched out a welcoming hand. 'Good for you, sir,' he said, as the youth was pulled and pushed up on to the stage.

There were preliminaries. The lad was taken behind the scenes and re-appeared, looking sheepish, stripped to his shirt, trousers and socks. Then the Tiger-Cat came on and they shook hands.

'Go it, Breezer!' shouted those in the audience who knew the unwilling challenger.

'Go it, Tiger-Cat!' yelled Kenneth, springing to his feet and leaping into the gangway.

'Interducin' Breezer Ben Trucket,' bellowed the fat man.

'Challengin' Tiger-Cat Bellamy Smith for the MAGNIFICENT purse of five jimmy o' goblins! Place your bets, gen'lemen sportsmen. Who'll have half-a-dollar on the Breezer?'

'Dollar and an'arf on the Cat,' shouted a voice from the back. The fat man smiled indulgently, shook his head, thanked the audience for their kind appreciation and gave a signal. A bell rang and the contest was on.

'Uncle Arthur,' I remember saying, 'has the Tiger-Cat changed his suit? He looks all shiny.'

'Greased all over,' Uncle Arthur replied. 'It's an old trick. That lad won't ever get a grip of him.'

The drunk, who had managed to get up, must have overheard this. Having risen to his feet, he wobbled uncertainly, supported himself by holding on to the shoulders of a small man in the row in front, gave a terrific belch and shouted out:

'He'sh oiled! The Cat'sh oiled! Drown that (hic!) Cat. He'sh oiled!'

'*You're* oiled!' called out someone near the front, turning round.

'Siddown, yer fool!' shouted others.

'Gen'lemen, *please*!' yelled the fat man, advancing once again to the front of the stage. 'Keep your seats, gen'lemen, *please*! Kindly keep your SEATS!'

At this critical moment the Tiger-Cat elected to become tactless. He abandoned the dodging and feinting with which he had been lulling the audience into a hope that Breezer Ben, the pride of whatever Oxfordshire village he came from, might actually win the five-pound prize, lifted him into the air, flung him down and appeared to jump on him. Ben forgot his manhood and gave a boyish squeal of agony. At this, his friends, who numbered at least half a dozen, most of them more than half-drunk, rushed the platform, knocking the fat man down.

The rest of the audience reacted according to their various natures. Some yelled, 'Siddown!' Others stamped on the ground and whistled through their fingers. One or two made for the exit. A tall, dark woman in the front row darted up the steps on to the platform and flung herself into the fray on behalf of the Tiger-Cat, who looked (grease or no grease) as though he was going to take a dreadful bashing from Ben's infuriated friends. The seconds rushed in and what Kipling would have called 'a mêlée of a sumptuous kind' ensued, with the dark woman in the thick of it.

Kenneth, still in the gangway, suddenly shrieked, 'It's Sukie! Leave her alone! Leave her alone, you beasts!' He ran towards the flight of steps. Uncle Arthur shoved me backwards, pushed past me and tore after him. A few moments later, with Kenneth tucked ignominiously under Uncle Arthur's arm and with myself in frightened but, all the same, unwilling tow, we left the now seething marquee and were just in time to see a couple of policemen approaching it. At the same moment Sukie and the Tiger-Cat crawled out from between two of the tent-pegs, spotted the policemen and snaked off into the gloom beyond the public house just as St Swithin's clock chimed the three-quarters to eleven.

We had much to tell Aunt Kirstie when we got home, but as soon as she had given us cocoa and biscuits she took us straight over, in the midst of our excited babbling, to Aunt Lally, who said,

'Well, I declare, Kirstie! Keeping them out till all hours and me out of my bed! Arthur ought to be ashamed of himself! Their grandfather went upstairs an hour or more ago, and what *he'll* say to them in the morning I *don't* know!'

'The fair comes only once a year and the bus before the last one didn't run, and the last was late,' said Aunt Kirstie, who never objected to telling any lies which seemed likely to improve a difficult situation. 'Besides, I kept 'em to give 'em a cup of cocoa and a biscuit to save you the trouble, so they can go straight up to bed.'

We made no objection to this, for, what with the unprecedentedly late hour and the unusual amount of excitement, we were tired out. Kenneth, in fact, had slept on Uncle Arthur's shoulder all the way home in the bus and both of us had found the long walk home from the bus stop infinitely tedious and fatiguing.

In the morning Kenneth said, 'Did you notice his ear was bleeding?'

'Whose?'

'The gypsy man, the Tiger-Cat. He's *her* man, you know. Her husband, or whatever it is. They don't get married properly, only over the tongs, but it's the same thing. I mean, they are allowed to have children, and all that.'

I changed the subject back again, as being more interesting.

'How do you know his ear was bleeding?'

'Saw it as they passed the pub lights. He mopped it and the bit of rag was all dark. Somebody in that fight must have pulled his earring out.'

'Did he have an earring?'

'Yes, of course. All gypsies have them. Besides, I saw how the light caught it when that first chap chucked him off the stage. I say, it was a pretty good show, wasn't it? Wonder whether Uncle Arthur has left us anything on their bedroom table?'

'We didn't ought to expect anything,' I said, 'not after him paying for all he did at the fair.'

But the Sunday morning treat was there as usual, this time in the form of chocolate cream rabbits.

'You didn't have your Saturday bath,' said Aunt Kirstie, 'and I can't give it you now with Sunday dinner to cook, and your uncle's taken the dogs out looking for Mr Ward. He never came home last night or the night before.'

CHAPTER 7

Margaret, Kenneth and Lionel

To our disgust, on the day after the fair we were pressurised into going to Sunday school again, but when we got there we found there were great compensations. The air was full of rumour and surmise, so much so that other children, including Our Sarah and her brother Ern, who, like ourselves, were not Sunday school minded, had turned up in force to share in the gossip and speculate upon the happenings of the previous night.

Owing to our late bedtime following our outing to the fair, it had been supposed that we would have what the aunts called 'a long lie-in' on Sunday morning, but we had been too anxious to find out what little treat, if any, was waiting for us on Aunt Kirstie's bedside table to waste time in bed. It was as we were rejoicing over the chocolate cream rabbits and digesting the information that Uncle Arthur and the whippets were out looking for Mr Ward, that the blow (as we thought it at the time) had fallen. It was Aunt Lally's doing, of course. She came over to Aunt Kirstie's to tell us to change our clothes.

'So you'll be going to Sunday school,' said Aunt Kirstie. 'Better you'd have stayed in bed until it was too late to send you, but, one way and another, Lally's right. Today you'd best be kept out of mischief and Sunday school's one way of doing it, seems to me.'

'But, Aunt Kirstie, we never get into mischief,' said Kenneth, who could usually wheedle her into letting him have his own way.

'Oh, no?' said Aunt Lally. 'Let me tell you your grandpa has seen the way them bars is prised apart in that there fence at the bottom of that old garden, so best you keep clear of him for a bit unless you wants to tell him a lot of wicked lies.' She took us back with her, and off to Sunday school we were sent. In front of the building, the old drill hall, there was a broad space of gravel and on this were assembled all the children of the village and even one or two loutish youths. Few wanted to attend Sunday school. Most wanted to listen to, augment and further spread the news of what came to be known as 'the sheepwash murder'.

We joined Our Sarah's faithful group and listened, horrified and ghoulishly excited, to her narrative. As we had come in halfway through it, Kenneth plucked up courage to say, at the first opportunity.

'Please, Our Sarah, do begin again. We've only just come, and we've got some news, too.'

'You 'ave, you young Oi say? Out weth et, then, else Oi ent agoen' to tell ee nothen.'

'Well, if there's been a murder, like you say, perhaps our Mr Ward did it.'

'Mester Ward? What, that old codger what leve weth your auntie? How jer know?'

'We don't *know*, but he's disappeared, so, if there's been a murder, he may be running away from the police.'

'Well, Oi never!'

'So *please* begin at the beginning and don't leave anything out.'

'Well,' began Our Sarah, nothing loth, it seemed, to repeat her effects in front of an audience still further augmented by a couple of our cousins, Uncle George's boy and girl, 'Oi goes down to the sheepwash thes mornen a-chasen after two lettle uns as was warnted to be cleaned up for Sunday, our young Bert 'aven shet hes bretches and dodgen off not to get an 'oiden from our dad what had an 'ead on hem after the bandsmen's booze-up yesterday folleren the percession and that, when what does Oi foind?'

'You foinds a p'liceman down the sheepwash,' replied a respectful voice from among her audience.

'Roight ee are. Oi foinds a p'liceman. And what else does Oi foind?'

'You foinds as the sheepwash and all about and around es railed off weth stakes and a lot of theck rope so's nobody can't get near et,' said another voice.

'So what does Oi do?'

'You asks the p'liceman ef he's seed your lettle neppers.'

'Roight again. So he says no and to keep 'em away and any other cheldren, too, 'cos et's no place for cheldren and the p'lice has their orders and to hop et. So what does Oi say to that?'

'You says, "Oo's ben murdered, then?"'

'And what do *he* say?'

'He says, "What do *you* know about et?"'

'So Oi says, "You tell *me* and Oi'll tell *you*." But then I sees two more on 'em comen down Loy Hell luggen a dark man atween 'em, so Oi says, "Et's them geppos, then, es et?" And what do he say to that?'

'He says, " 'Op et, 'cos your guess es as good as moine and you are obstructen me in the course of moi dooty, so sleng your 'ook and don't come yer no more."'

'So then what does Oi do?'

'You pokes your tongue out at hem and then you sees your lettle neppers and you cotches up weth them and you cleans up Bert weth some long grass and washes hem off in the brook and runs 'em both home and tells your dad about the murder whoile your mam feneshes up cleanen young Bert at the ketchen senk.'

At this moment the Sunday school superintendent came out and rang a handbell and ordered us all inside the building, but Our Sarah said to her group,

'Oi ent agoen en there. Let's go down the sheepwash and see what's doen.'

'Can't, in our Sunday clothes,' said Kenneth. 'Besides, our

cousins would know and they'd split on us. I think we'd better go in.'

'*I* shan't,' I said, as I noticed our cousins and several others sneaking away towards the gate. 'I'm never going in there again after what that man said to me last time. I vote we walk up to the big house and try to get a word with Lionel. He won't have heard about the murder and I want to be the first to tell him, *and* to tell him about Mr Ward because he's a relation.'

'You don't really think Mr Ward is a murderer, do you?'

'He might even be the person who *got* murdered. Anyway, coming with me?'

'All right. We'd better go by way of The Marsh and up Lovers' Lane, so as not to go past Aunt Kirstie's.'

'We can't go up Lovers' Lane if the police have roped off the sheepwash. They might arrest us.'

'Not they. They can only send us away.'

'We're not supposed to use Lovers' Lane, anyway, and we've done one bad thing already, not going into Sunday school.'

'You can take a horse to Sunday school but you can't make it sing hymns,' said Kenneth.

We giggled at this witticism and passed out at the Sunday school gate. As we reached Mother Honour's shop Kenneth looked across the road at the tumbledown cottage and said,

'I suppose Mr Ward couldn't be hiding in there? Let's go and look.'

'Oh, come on,' I said. 'We can't go into that filthy place in our Sunday clothes.' So we crossed over at Mother Honour's, avoided the cottage and went on to The Marsh by way of the bridge and the culvert. It was, I suppose, less than half a mile to the sheepwash and long before we got there we could see several people standing about, but none of them looked like policemen.

'Might be detectives in plain clothes,' said Kenneth.

'One of them's Uncle Arthur,' I said, for I could see the two dogs. 'We'd better go back. We don't want questions asked about Sunday school.'

But the dogs had spotted us. Floss was on a lead; Vicky, who could be trusted, was not. She came leaping and bounding up to us and Uncle Arthur turned round to order her back and saw us.

'It's a fair cop,' muttered Kenneth, as he stooped to fondle Vicky. 'What shall we say?'

As it happened, there was no need to say anything, for Uncle Arthur either had forgotten or did not realise that we ought to have been in Sunday school. Later we remembered that he had not been present when we received our marching orders.

'You two get off home,' he said. 'No place for children, this isn't.'

'Why isn't it?' I asked, playing the innocent. I noticed, incidentally, that the ropes and stakes which Our Sarah had mentioned were no longer in position and that the bystanders were neither policemen nor detectives, but Sunday morning idlers come to gawp at the spot marked with a cross.

'Something happened last night to a poor young girl,' said Uncle Arthur, 'so you mind what your dad and mam tells you, and don't you ever go speaking to no strangers.'

'We never do,' I said, forgetting for the moment that once Kenneth had spoken to Old Sukie. We fell in beside Uncle Arthur and when we reached grandfather's little wooden bridge over the brook, our uncle indicated it and told us to cut off home. This did not fit in with our plans at all, but we crossed the planks, opened the iron gate and walked a little way up the path between the currant bushes. When we snaked back to the gate and cautiously opened it, Uncle Arthur was almost up to the culvert. We watched him cross the little bridge and disappear round the corner. He had taken the road which led away from the village and, indeed, had he planned to return home, he would have accompanied us.

'He's killing time until the pub opens at twelve,' said Kenneth, 'then he'll go in and ask the men if they've seen Mr Ward. I reckon we've got at least a couple of hours.'

'We haven't, you know,' I said. 'Sunday school comes out at eleven to be ready for church. We'll be expected home.'

'We can say we went for a walk.'

'What! When Uncle Arthur thinks we went straight home when he left us?'

'Oh, well, perhaps we'd better just hang about until Sunday school comes out, then, and look in on Aunt Kirstie just to get ourselves identified and then we can go off again. She'll be too busy with the Sunday roast to bother about what we're up to, and dinner isn't on the table until half-past one, so how about that?'

'How will we know when Sunday school is over?'

'We'll have to get back there and join the others as they come out.'

'Suppose we're spotted getting there?'

'We won't be. All we've got to do is nip past Polly's stable, get through the fence, nip through the hermit's cottage and sneak past Mrs Honour's.'

'That's if there's nobody in the cottage. Suppose Mr Ward is in there again! And it's such a mess!'

'Have to chance it. Come on,' said Kenneth, 'and look out for that frock of yours. We don't want questions asked about damage to Sunday clothes.'

'Just the reason I said before. I don't want to go to that cottage,' I said. 'It's so filthy.'

'Suit yourself. I'll go alone, then, and come back here and give you the tip when Sunday school is out.'

But this was too much for my elder-sisterly pride.

'Oh, come on, then,' I said crossly and, without another word, we made our way past the stable and squeezed through between the widened bars in the hermit's backyard fence.

We stood a moment, listening, but there was not a sound in the weedy, overgrown garden, not a bird-note, not even a scurrying rat. The silence, indeed, was uncanny and I think we both felt we ought not to break it. It was an enchantment, but an uncomfortable one. I remember thinking of a ghost-story I had read where the most sinister ghosts were not confined to the hours of darkness, but stalked the earth, tall and terrible as the Host of the Sidh, at noonday at the full zenith of the sun.

There was no wind, either, not so much as the sigh of a

zephyr, and my thoughts took another although not a more comforting turn.

'It's like Walter de la Mare,' I said softly, for my class had had an enlightened young teacher the previous term, a student from a London college, who took us once a week for poetry.

'It's like where someone has died,' said Kenneth. 'Let's leave. The place gives me the creeps.'

There was only one major change inside the stinking, grisly little cottage. Somebody had filled in Mr Ward's grave-like hole and stamped the earth flat over it. His pickaxe was leaning up against a filthy wall, but his spade had gone. We heard later that the police had found it at the bottom of the deepest part of the sheepwash.

No questions were asked regarding Sunday school, but this did not surprise us much. Very little notice was ever taken of our doings so long as we did not get openly into mischief and very little interest was displayed in those things which interested us. This was not owing to negligence, but simply to the fact that, so long as we ate heartily, were what the aunts termed 'biddable' and did not appear to be sickening for anything, our welfare, both physical and spiritual, was taken for granted —a state of affairs which suited everybody, ourselves included.

Sunday dinner—it was roast loin of pork and I was given a chop with a bit of delicious kidney in it—was over at a quarter to three and, as usual, we were sent next door to Aunt Lally to do our Sunday reading of improving literature. As, like Aunt Kirstie and Uncle Arthur, Aunt Lally retired to her bed until Sunday tea-time, we never found much difficulty in slipping out of the house without waking grandfather, whose custom it was to put a large handkerchief over his face and sleep in his armchair until Aunt Lally woke him to give him his tea. When she reappeared she always found us piously perusing the books and pamphlets she had left with us and I will say for her that she never catechised us upon what we were supposed to have read. From her point of view, it was easier not to do so than to involve us in lies or to hear our unpalatable truths. I cannot really believe she thought we had spent the best part of two hours in reading 'How Paul's penny became a pound' or 'Little Meg's Children', let alone the tracts and other moralistic works of which she had such a collection, but she was a simple soul, so perhaps she did think we were as good as I am sure we appeared to be.

On this particular Sunday afternoon we gave her a good quarter of an hour to get settled upstairs and for grandfather to begin his gentle snoring, then we crept down the back stairs to the scullery and left by the back door. We had no fear of encountering Uncle Arthur or Aunt Kirstie. They, too, would have retired upstairs until it was tea-time. It was most grown-ups' invariable custom on Sundays.

As we walked up the hill to the manor house we discussed how best to get hold of Lionel and decided to try the garden first. If he was not there, the next best thing, we thought, would be to knock at the back door and enquire for him, as it would probably be answered by one of the maids, whereas the front door would be opened by the overpowering, supercilious, majestic butler.

As it happened, we were lucky. Lionel was down by the pond chucking stones, of which he appeared to have collected a fair-sized heap from the gravel drive, into the water. He seemed pleased to see us, although he informed us that it might mean saying goodbye, as he was forbidden to go into the village.

'It's this murder,' he said. 'There are policemen up at the house this very minute. They've been here all day questioning people. I don't suppose you know about it yet, but there's been a murder on The Marsh.'

'Of course we know. Everybody knows. But why should police come here?' asked Kenneth. 'Has one of you done the murder?' (Of course he was thinking of Mr Ward.)

'I shouldn't imagine so, but we don't really know. You remember my sister had a birthday party yesterday? Well, one of the guests went out and got herself killed. That's why the police are here,' explained Lionel.

'The body was found down by the sheepwash,' said Kenneth.

'So you do know about it! I'll tell you something you *don't* know, though. Well, anyway, I *bet* you don't. You don't know what she was wearing when she was killed. Want to see?'

'Don't be silly,' I said. 'You're just being cocky. The police wouldn't let *you* have whatever she was wearing. They would keep it for clues and things.'

'You don't know everything,' said Lionel. 'Come on. I'll show you. I ought to charge you something, but I don't suppose you have any money, have you?'

'Spent it all at the fair.'

'Oh, what was the fair like? Was it any good?'

'Fabulous. Uncle Arthur won a cigar and a coconut and we saw some wrestling and there was a fight and we didn't get home till after midnight. What are you going to show us?'

'Come and see. We'll sneak in by the side door and use the back staircase. Don't speak a word or make any kind of a row until we're in my playroom with the door shut.'

We crept in past the pantry, mounted the servants' staircase and tip-toed along to the attics which were Lionel's domain. He took us into the playroom, shut the door and disappeared into his bedroom. In a few minutes one of the hideous and frightful creatures which had collected for charity in the village on Saturday came prancing into the room.

I clapped a hand over my mouth to stifle an involuntary cry as the creature pirouetted towards us and I recoiled from it, putting out my other hand to fend it off. Kenneth dodged over to the bedroom door and gently closed it. Then he said,

'How did you manage to get those things?'

Lionel danced about a bit more and then shrugged himself out of the lendings which he laid carefully on the only armchair in the room.

'I managed to get them because I sneaked them and wouldn't give them back,' he said.

'Off the body? I don't believe a word of it,' said Kenneth.

'Of course not off the body. These are duplicates. There were two of each costume and I picked the one I thought might fit. Doctor Tassall brought them from the hospital in a wagonette. Amabel got Grandmamma to hire it and buy the costumes for the party. When they came they were laid out in the dining-room, so I took one for myself and in the end I was allowed to keep it because I wasn't going to the party and had to go to bed early. So they all tried on their costumes for size, you know, and this girl who got murdered had the one like this. I wore mine, on and off, most of the evening until my bed-time. I went round with my money-box cadging sixpences from the guests when Grandmamma wasn't about. Then, when they were dressing for the charades, this girl came up here with her costume and asked me if I would mind swopping over with her, as she thought my costume might be a bit roomier than hers. She was a fairly fat person, you see, and actually rather plain. As a matter of fact, she hadn't been invited to the party, but she brought three others in her brother's car, so, of course, she had to be asked to stay. My sister was a bit annoyed about it, because the person who *should* have brought the other three girls was the brother, but he had to cry off at the last minute because he'd crocked his knee or something. My sister didn't want another girl, especially such a plain girl as that, so she made a scene to Grandmamma and Grandmamma was a good bit sick with her.'

'So did you swop costumes with this girl?'

'Oh, yes. It suited me all right. The only difference in the costumes was the size, so far as I could see, except one was more brown and the other was more green, and the masks were a bit different, that's all. Nothing, really. Anyway, she offered me half-a-crown to swop, so it was worth it.'

'But that means,' said Kenneth, 'that the wrong person got murdered.'

'What wrong person?'

'Well, you, I suppose the murder was meant for.'

'Oh, shucks. I was in bed at that time.'

'Well, have the police questioned you as well as the others?'

'Oh, yes, but I couldn't tell them anything except that we'd swopped the costumes.'

Kenneth and I held a deep discussion as we walked homewards down the hill.

'She was mistaken for Lionel,' said Kenneth. 'I'm certain of it. She wasn't even supposed to be at the party.'

'But who would want to murder Lionel? He's only a boy,' I argued.

'The princes in the Tower were only boys, but they were in somebody's way and perhaps Lionel is, too.'

'Whose way could he be in?'

'Mr Ward's, of course. Don't you remember Lionel telling us that the big house, and all that, would be his when he was twenty-one?'

'So what?'

'Well, if Mr Ward is a relation, perhaps it would all be his if Lionel was out of the way.'

I was immensely impressed by this.

'No wonder Lionel's parents won't let him come down to the village any more,' I said. 'It's sickening for him, but I don't blame them. They must think he's still in danger.'

'Well, I expect he is. Murderers don't stick at much, and if Mr Ward is a murderer and can get that house and everything by killing Lionel, I expect he will.'

'Lionel ought to be guarded night and day,' I said.

'Are you volunteering?' Kenneth enquired.

'We couldn't do much against a murderer.'

'We could yell the place down, I suppose, if we saw him collaring Lionel.'

'A fat lot of use *that* would be. The murderer would simply murder us, too, to shut our mouths. That's what murderers always do. It's in the Sunday papers,' I said.

We decided to leave Lionel to his fate. Aunt Lally found us deep in *Moments of Meditation* and *Little Thoughts of Great Men* when she came downstairs at five and sent us off to Aunt Kirstie to be given our Sunday tea.

CHAPTER 8

Mrs Kempson Again

It is so kind of you, dear Mrs Bradley, to agree to come down here, but as you will see from what follows, at present it would be nothing but a waste of your very valuable time. Ward is no longer here. He seems to have walked out of his lodgings last Friday and has completely disappeared. The Landgraves, with whom he was domiciled, informed me of what had happened, and, of course, they do not know how to trace him and are upset at losing what I suppose has been a welcome source of income. Neither is that by any means the worst of it.

Ward's disappearance, provided it could be permanent, would be a relief to me, but, in view of what has happened, I can obtain no satisfaction from it. In fact, the reverse is the case. I am filled with misgivings and am only too conscious that very soon my misgivings may give place to something not far removed from actual trepidation. Let me relate the circumstances so far as they are known to me at present.

They appear to stem from a party which I gave for Amabel, my grand-daughter, little Lionel's sister, on her nineteenth birthday which she celebrated on Saturday. The arrangements were made before she left her finishing school in Paris and it seemed reasonable to me that the list of guests should be compiled by Amabel herself. She sent me the names and addresses of her friends and I issued the invitations personally.

Quite a number of the guests lived in London, where Amabel's parents have a flat at which the family stay when they are in England, so the names on Amabel's list were almost all of them unknown to me, but this occasioned me no uneasiness, since I knew (or thought I did) that Amabel was a good, sensible girl who would be unlikely to make undesirable acquaintances and still more unlikely to invite any such to my house. I ought to add that nobody living in my vicinity appeared to have been invited, or I should have instituted enquiries. That I was deceived you will learn as you read on. I am bitterly disappointed in Amabel, and have told her so, but she claims that the address in question was valid when she sent it to me. I refer, of course, to the London address of Doctor Tassall.

Against Amabel's wishes, I insisted upon receiving her guests in formal fashion. I stood at the head of the staircase with her beside me and I had Barker announce each arrival. Among them was this young man, Doctor Noel Tassall. When I read his name on Amabel's list I had no idea that he was Doctor Matters' new assistant—not that I employ Doctor Matters, of course; I go to a London man whom I have known for years—but I had taken it for granted that Doctor Tassall's was an academic title and that he was one of Amabel's former teachers, since, against my better judgment, she had been taught, up to her eighteenth year, at a co-educational boarding school where half the staff were men.

I recognised Doctor Tassall, of course, as soon as he mounted the stairs, for I had seen him riding his horse in the village, but it had never occurred to me to find out his name and I cannot remember who it was who first pointed him out to me and told me that he had come to assist Doctor Matters, an elderly man and not, I would think, really up to his work, although probably he still retains enough knowledge and energy to deal with the village ailments and deliver the village babies.

This, however, is beside the point. The fact of the matter is that, all the time I was at the party—I left it and retired to my room at ten—I noticed that Amabel danced almost entirely with this eminently unsuitable young man and that their attitude towards one another was warm, informal and, not to mince words, far more intimate and exclusive than could possibly meet with my approval. At the first opportunity I spoke to her.

'You are neglecting your other guests,' I said. She was flushed and smiling. She gave me a swift peck on the cheek.

'Oh, don't be stuffy, darling,' she said. 'Anyway, he expects to be called out to a confinement at any minute, so not to worry.'

'How do you come to know Doctor Tassall?' I asked.

'Can't remember. Met him in London somewhere. Ah, here he comes with some provender. I must say, Grandmamma, you've done me proud with the fodder and horse-trough.' (Such language from a girl!)

It was soon after this that I retired to my room and had my maid put me to bed. I knew that my room was sufficiently far from the revels to be free of their raucous sounds and the last I remember of the party was when I heard one of the young women suggest that they play charades. Amabel said,

'All right. The girls can have my room to dress up in, and the men—may they use yours, Nigel?'

My dear adopted boy, of course, was present at the beginning of the party and I am bound to say that his conduct was in marked contrast to that of Amabel. He mixed with the others, danced in turn with the young women and in every way comported himself with dignity and discretion. He consented to allow his den to be used as a dressing-room for the male guests and before sides could be picked for the charades Doctor Tassall was called away. My daughter and her husband had left the hall earlier, explaining to me that the young people would be happier on their own. If this was meant as a hint to me to follow their example, it failed of its object. I thought that a certain amount of supervision was desirable, but at mention of charades I decided that, as I was feeling tired and as this new activity was innocent and innocuous enough but would probably be extremely noisy, I was justified in seeking a little well-earned peace and quiet. I left word with Barker to lock up when everybody had gone and I went to bed. I took my tablet and fell asleep almost at once.

My sleep, however, did not last very long. What woke me I do not know, unless it was a premonition that all was not well.

I leaned up on my elbow and listened. I could hear nothing except a soft sound of scuffling just outside my door. Then a girl's voice said: 'Stop it, you fool! There might be somebody asleep in there!'

I switched on the light and rang my night-bell. After what I considered to be an unnecessary delay, my maid came in,

'Bridges,' I said, 'who is that on the landing?'

'Landing, madam?'

'Two persons have been scuffling about on the landing outside my room. Ask them to go downstairs at once!'

'There's nobody outside your door, madam. I would have seen them as I come along the corridor.'

'Well, anyway, it is time the party began to break up,' I said. 'Go downstairs and take my instructions to Mr Nigel. He will know how to cope. I don't want people here after midnight. After all, tomorrow is Sunday. Besides, most of these young people have to get back to London.'

She returned after about ten minutes.

'Mr Nigel isn't there, madam. Miss Amabel tells me as he had arranged to pick up the photographer at eleven, there being no other way of getting him here so late excepting by car.'

'Oh, yes, I remember,' I said. 'Well, he should not be long. Tell Barker to have a word with him directly he gets back. As soon as the photographer has taken the groups, the party is to close down.'

'Very good, madam.'

I settled myself once more, secure in the knowledge that Nigel was to be relied on to respect my wishes and also the sanctity of the Sabbath. I was sorry, all the same, that he had had to absent himself from the party, for I thought it would take him more than an hour to drive into the town, pick up the photographer and return here, and I was not anxious to give Amabel and her friends *carte blanche* while they were unsupervised. I thought of sending Bridges to find Harlow

Conyers and my daughter and request them to take charge, but I feared it would be useless, as, from the beginning, they had not been in favour of superintending the party. It was only because of my insistence upon their presence that they had been persuaded to attend it.

I fell asleep again at last and exactly how long I slept I do not know. I was awakened by a tapping at my door, followed by the entrance of Bridges in her dressing-gown.

'Madam,' she said, 'there's a bit of a schemozzle downstairs, and the gentlemen told Barker to tell me to let you know.'

'A *what*?' I said sharply. 'What on earth do you mean?'

'One of the young ladies went out to get a breath of air more than three hours ago, madam, and hasn't never come back,' she explained, looking excited and important, as servants do when they suspect that they are the bearers of ill-tidings or a breath of scandal.

'What of it?' I asked crossly. 'I suppose she has tired of the party and gone home.'

'It is not hardly thought so, madam. Seems some of them got too warm after the bits of play-acting, madam, and went out, but nobody don't think as she has gone home, seeing as how it seems she was still in her fancy dress, one of them costumes as the gentlemen students wore for the charity parade this morning in the village.'

'Still in her fancy dress? But why? What makes you think so?'

'Miss Amabel says as the clothes she come here in, madam, is still in the bedroom.'

'But whatever can have possessed her to go out in that hideous masquerade?'

'Something to do with the photographs, madam, it's thought. Miss Amabel said as they was to keep them on.'

'Oh, of course! They were to be taken wearing these monstrosities.'

'It seems they was hot to wear, madam, so this young lady says as she would just take a turn up the drive, but she hasn't never come back in again. Doctor Tassall, what was called out on a case before you retired, madam, come back about one o'clock, but says he never saw her on the drive, nor did Mr Nigel, who come in just a while ago, which he reckons he would have picked her out if she'd of been there, so Mr Nigel and them are talking about a search-party, madam, and mention was made of them gypsies up the hill, madam.'

'Oh, nonsense!' I exclaimed. 'What would gypsies be doing in my grounds? Anyhow, which of the girls is it?'

'It's the young lady which, as you know, madam, come in a car with three other young ladies and was not in her party dress, madam, and the car is still here, madam. Besides, Mr Nigel says you couldn't get one of them horrible costumes into a car because you couldn't sit down in it, and she couldn't hardly have took it off, madam, because Miss Amabel says as her clothes is still here, like I said, and I knows for a fact as the young ladies was all stripped down to their undies, madam. She wouldn't have took the fancy costume off without coming back to the house, madam, and that's what her friends say she certainly has not done, madam.'

'Oh, dear! How very tiresome people are! I suppose I had better go down,' I said.

She helped me to dress and down I went, not in the best of tempers at this disturbance of my night's rest. Except for one young man who was sitting on the floor with his head against the wall, obviously in a drunken slumber, the guests who were left looked sober and anxious enough.

Nigel came up to me. Doctor Tassall was with him.

'Sorry about this, darling,' he said. 'You go back to bed. Tassall and I will cope. I'm organising a search-party. Ten to one the silly wench has gone and twisted her ankle or something of that sort. Not to worry. Maybe somebody ought to have gone looking for her sooner, but some of them were a trifle under the influence and I suppose they were all enjoying themselves, so I don't think anybody noticed she was missing until about half-an-hour ago. I've had the house pretty well combed, but she isn't here.'

'I shall wait up until your search-party returns,' I said. 'I cannot imagine what the foolish girl was thinking of, to go wandering away at this hour of the morning.'

'I'm afraid people have been very remiss, darling,' he said. 'It wasn't "this hour of the morning" when she stepped out. She's been missing since about eleven o'clock. If only that damned photographer had turned up, we should have realised she wasn't with us, but, of course, he didn't show up, although I waited for an hour in Broad Street, where I'd arranged to meet him.'

'Photographer?' I said. 'Oh, yes, of course. Amabel wanted photographs, didn't she? Did he not appear?'

'Not even his astral body. I suppose they kept him so long at that County Councillors' dinner, or whatever his other assignment was, that he thought it was too late to meet me and come on here. It wasn't until the other three girls decided it was time to pile into their car and go home, that they realised their driver was missing.'

'I can't think why they did not realise it much earlier,' I said. 'They knew, I suppose, that she had left the house.'

'I understand that, after the charades, most people went on to the terrace to cool off,' said young Doctor Tassall.

'That's right,' said another young man. 'Amabel wouldn't let us take off the lendings because of the photographer. Most of us went outside for a breath of air, so she wouldn't have been missed for a bit. Then people sort of drifted in again and hung about because, I mean, you couldn't *dance* in those fancy outfits, and after that I'm afraid there was a bit of hunting in couples and people sneaked away upstairs and took the costumes off, don't you know, and so forth. You couldn't really say, at any given time, where *anybody* was, and that's the strength of it, so she wouldn't really have been missed at all, you see.'

'I cannot understand what Harlow and Esmée were thinking about, to walk away from the party the way they did, and go off without a thought for their responsibilities. After all, Amabel is their daughter,' I said angrily.

'Well, darling,' said Nigel, with an unpalatable degree of truth, 'isn't that a case of the pot calling the kettle black? It's *your* house, after all, and *you* walked out and left the revellers to it, just as they did. It's a great pity that Tassall and I both had to be out of the house at the same time. As for that damned photographer, I could wish him at Jericho and Tassall's expectant mother, too! Anyway, we're going to search the grounds. The wretched girl can't be all that far away!'

CHAPTER 9

Letters

Mrs Kempson's Letter Continued

From this point onwards, my dear Mrs Bradley, my letter may appear somewhat incoherent, but I will be as lucid as I can. Some of the remaining men claimed that they must escort their sisters or female friends home and would therefore be unavailable as members of a search-party. This seemed to me reasonable enough at that hour of the morning, so, in the end, the searchers were reduced to three: my son-in-law Harlow Conyers, my beloved Nigel and Amabel's friend, young Doctor Tassall, who immediately and rightly stated that, if the girl had suffered an injury, he would be of more use than anybody else.

They were about to leave the house with the only two electric torches we could muster, when Lionel came down in his pyjamas and dressing-gown and wanted to know what was happening. He demanded to be allowed to join the search-party, but, of course, this was out of the question. He then stated that he possessed a powerful torch and was sent upstairs to fetch it and be prepared to lend it to Doctor Tassall. This he did and, as a reward, was told by his father that he might stay up for a while, which he elected to do. As soon as they had gone, he put on the fearsome fancy dress which he had commandeered when the costumes arrived. It was that of an *iguanadon*, or so he informed me.

He then settled down and gave me a lecture on prehistoric

animals, which passed the time until we received further news. I was glad of the child's company, for I had a premonition that something very serious had happened. At last my son-in-law presented himself and looked taken aback at the sight of his young son. He sent him straight back to bed and seemed angry with him. I could see that something else was the matter, and I looked anxiously at Harlow, who, after all, had given permission for Lionel to stay up.

'Has she hurt herself?' I asked, when the child had gone.

'Yes, badly, I'm afraid. I came on ahead to tell you. The doctor and Nigel are bringing her in.'

'How bad is it?' I asked.

'Worse than bad,' said Harlow. 'We're in for trouble, mater. The poor girl has copped it.'

'Do you mean—you don't mean—rape?' I asked, my thoughts flying in horror to the gypsy encampment on Lye Hill, although previously I had dismissed such an idea.

'That remains to be discovered,' said Harlow grimly. 'Take hold on yourself, mater. The primary fact we have to face is that the poor kid is dead.'

'Dead?' I said, in stupid repetition of the unbelievable word.

He nodded. 'I'd better go back and help them along with her,' he said. 'I thought you ought to know, though, before they bring her into the house. Will you ring the police?'

'The police?' I echoed, stupidly again.

'Yes, of course. We mustn't delay. Ring them at once.'

'But what shall I tell them?'

'That we have to report the finding of a girl's body near the sheepwash at the foot of Lye Hill. Just tell them that. All further information can wait until they arrive.' He went off and I did as he suggested. The police asked on the telephone whether we knew the girl's identity. I replied that we did, and was told that they would be along immediately and that nothing was to be touched. I indicated that this was nonsense and that the body, as the girl was a guest of mine, would be brought to the house, but the policeman at the other end, having given his orders, had rung off.

I sat and waited. At the end of about an hour Harlow

returned. I told him what the police had said. He nodded.

'Just as well we had young Tassall with us,' he said. 'Told us the very same thing. He and Nigel are standing by.'

'But, surely, in a case of accidental death...'

'Accidental nothing, mater.'

'What on earth do you mean?' I felt myself beginning to tremble and my head to swim.

'Tassall thinks she's been attacked.'

'Not—oh, no! *No!*' I cried.

'Steady on, mater. We've got to face facts.'

'But if she's been attacked—and is dead—'

'That's it,' he said. 'Murder. Not very nice for us, is it? What on earth possessed her to leave the drive and go right down Lovers' Lane at such an hour? We shall never know, I suppose, but there it is. Sit down, mater. I'll get you a drop of brandy.'

Well, Mrs Bradley, the poor child's body was never brought to the house. The police, when they had made their preliminary investigation, had it taken to the mortuary in the town and as I had the girl's home address and telephone number (since it was I, as hostess, who had issued the invitations to the birthday party, although the original invitation had been sent to the girl's brother) I was able to get in touch with the relatives.

I do not think I closed my eyes that night or, rather, early morning, and later in the morning, of course, the police came again. They wanted the names and addresses of everybody who had been present at the party. They were very polite, but very inquisitive.

What kind of party? List of guests? Drinks? Drugs? Quarrels? Rivalries? Jealousies?

Really, Mrs Bradley, you cannot imagine!

It was not that kind of party, I assured them. The young people had been dancing and playing at charades and the girl in question, Merle Patterson, had said she was going out for a breath of air. Others did the same, but nobody else went further than the terrace.

Was I sure of that?

No, not to be able to swear to it, but so I had been informed.

Had the girl come with a male escort?

No. She had been one of a party of four, all old girls of my grand-daughter's previous school.

And so on and so forth. Everybody in the house was questioned, and this included the servants. Just as the inspector had released me from his mesmerism—for, indeed, I was quite bemused by this lengthy interrogation—my butler informed me that Mrs Landgrave from the village was asking to speak to me.

'Oh, send her away,' I said. 'She must come at some more convenient time. I can't see her now. Ask her to leave a message if it's anything to do with Mr Ward.'

Well, it was! Ward had not returned to his lodgings for the past two nights and Mrs Landgrave thought I ought to be told.

One dreadful detail has been brought to our notice. The police believe they have found the weapon the murderer used. A heavy spade had been thrown into the deepest part of the sheepwash and the nature of the poor girl's injuries—but, no! I cannot go on! We are living in a nightmare. I do hope you have not altered your plans in order to come here, but you will understand that for you to visit us at present would be a waste of your time.

Doctor Tassall's Letter

By this time you will have heard our bad news. It never occurred to me, dear godfather, that when you encouraged me to study medicine I should be called as a witness at the inquest on a case of murder, but so it has proved. Mrs Kempson, into whose well-ordered, not to say snobbish and sheltered, existence some rain has now fallen for the first time, I fancy, since the death of her husband, let your name drop at some time during that ill-fated birthday party, but I did not let on that I knew you, as I feared she would not believe me. As I am hoping to become her grandson-in-law, I did not want to antagonise her more than I could help and I thought that for me to claim acquaintanceship, not to say godsonship, with so eminent a personage as yourself might cause her to think me even more of a mountebank than she does at present. Besides, she would be bound to find out (unless you will reinstate me in your good graces) that you have banned me from your house since I told you I had broken with my little blackbird, Merle, and wanted to marry Amabel Kempson-Conyers.

First I ought to explain about Amabel, and this is where I throw myself, dear godfather, on your mercy. She is a beautiful young hussy whom I encountered under romantic circumstances a year ago in Paris, where I was celebrating the lucky fluke which enabled me, at the end of my course, to put the magic letters M.B. after my name.

She and another rash child were playing hooky from their finishing school one evening when they were accosted by a couple of amorous French youths of undesirable type. I contrived to break up the little party by claiming to be Amabel's brother and suggesting that I should whistle for the gendarmes if the boys did not abandon their obvious intentions. One of them pulled a knife, so I laid him out, took the girls back to their home from home, expressed the hope that both would receive a sound spanking from the dragon-in-charge and handed them over to the *concierge* with a large bribe to persuade her not to give them away.

That, I supposed, would be the end of it, but this was not to be. No, I'll be honest, godfather. I hoped it *wouldn't* be the end of it, so, having extracted from the young delinquents on the way home the information that they were in the first weeks of their year at finishing-school, I began to haunt the Sights of Paris in the hope of catching up with Amabel again.

It came off in the Louvre. Half-a-dozen young beazels, all demureness and devilment, were being towed around the galleries by a couple of grim, black-clad females of official aspect and, directly she spotted me, Amabel gave a slight squeal, grabbed one of the females, chattered away in French, broke ranks and, seizing my hands, kissed me fervently on both cheeks, rushed me up to the rest of the gang and introduced me as her brother(!).

After that, it was all gas and gaiters—nothing to it. I wrote her a prim, brotherly letter in case their mail was censored, received a reply, and that was the beginning of the end; at least, I hope so, for I intend to marry her. She needs a firm hand and I am the man to supply it. Unfortunately, if I make known (at this stage) my intentions, honourable though they are, there is the chance that old Mrs Kempson will persuade the parents to make Amabel a ward of court and rob me, no doubt, of access to her, unless I fancy a spell in chokey which, quite frankly, dear godfather, I most emphatically do not.

Well, to our muttons. As you know, I returned from Paris to take up a post as assistant and general dogsbody to old Doctor Faustus (I call him that, because you never saw anything like his dispensary except in bad dreams) but, naturally, I kept in touch with Amabel and she with me. I knew, therefore, the date of her return to England and that she proposed to make a lengthy stay at Hill House, so, to disclose a truth which you will not need to be told, I only took the Faustus job to be near her in the village where her ancestral hall dominates the hilltop.

We managed to meet two or three times in London after she first got back, and then I received an invitation to the birthday party. It was from old Mrs Kempson herself, and I don't know how Amabel wangled it. However, I put on a clean shirt and showed up.

On the morning of the party there was a charity rag led by some of the University Medical School fellows. Apparently they called at the Big House and then nothing would satisfy Amabel but to borrow or buy the prehistoric-animal costumes in which they appeared. She got a message to me at the surgery by way of one of her grandmother's servants, so as soon as I was free I engaged the lads on the blower and arranged for a wagonette of obsolete vintage to deliver the costumes to the manor. From what I heard later, young Lionel, Amabel's kid brother, watched the costumes being unloaded and immediately claimed one for himself. More about that later.

Meanwhile, I suppose you wouldn't care to come along and hear me give my evidence, such as it is, to the coroner? I feel I shall do you credit in the witness box, although the thunder, I suspect, will be stolen by the police doctor, who will be in the enviable position of one to whom the city mortuary is his washpot, not to mention that over the police-station hath he cast out his shoe.

Incidentally, although she's probably too stiff-necked to say so, I believe Mrs Kempson could do with a bit of support from you. She isn't very young and the knowledge that a guest at her party has been slugged and killed in the immediate neighbourhood of her ancestral home has given her more than somewhat of a jolt. Apart from that, your presence (especially if you would be willing to drop a word in my favour) would give me enormous pleasure.

Amabel Kempson-Conyers' Letter

Oh, Maisy, how I wish it had never occurred to me to buy those wretched lizard-costume things from the boys at the medical school! And how lucky you are that Anthony insisted on taking you home so early. I suppose you went to his flat in his car and whooped it up a bit. Not that I'm jealous, darling. Your Amabel has her own bit of cake stashed away and is perfectly content with it.

Still, never mind that. No doubt our troubles will be a nine-days' wonder in the papers, but I'd like to give you *my* version because, maybe, to write it down will clear my head in case I'm called upon to give evidence at the inquest, as I think I'm bound to be. I'm sure the whole thing is connected with those prehistoric things. Do you think there's a curse on them or something?

Anyway, this is what has happened. You remember how we shared out the costumes, I expect? They—that's to say, the rag students—were limited in their ideas because each of them had to have an outfit which only involved two legs, unless anybody was willing either to have a partner, like a pantomime horse, or else go about on all fours which, for dashing about the town and village collecting for charity, simply was not feasible.

So, as I say, the restrictions. Not everybody got a costume, because the students could only supply fourteen costumes altogether. Each one was labelled as to what it was supposed to be. Well, owing to the limitations of only needing the two-legged types of pre-historic monsters, each costume was duplicated and there were only the fourteen altogether, of which my wretched little brother Lionel bagged one as soon as they were unpacked and refused to give it back. He bore it off, cavorted about in it until, mercifully, he was sent to bed, and we did not see it downstairs again until after two o'clock in the morning, after you and Anthony had sneaked off without saying goodbye.

My first idea had been to pair off people as male and female of the same species, but when I looked at the costumes I saw that this was impossible because some of the things were too heavy and too bulky for us poor females to manage, so, in the event, as you may or may not recollect, we had two men as *Tyrannosaurus*, two, rather similar, as *Tarbosaurus* and two as *Corythosaurus*, a terribly silly-looking creature with a huge duckbill and a sort of helmet on its head. We gave those to Chris and Billy, if you remember, so that they could clown a bit, which I knew they would do, anyway. It makes them a bit tiresome at times, but, being so beetle-brained, I suppose they have to give some scope to their ego, although they can be fatiguing. I specially think so after my rather *sophisticated* year in Paris, meeting French boys, who are ardent without being silly and have beautiful manners so long as you don't give them too much encouragement, but, on the whole, I would rather trust Chris and Billy, in spite of their lunatic antics. Of course we didn't get much chance of encouraging the French boys, as we were very well chaperoned—talk about Spanish duennas!—but there's always a way.

Oh, well, that's not what I'm writing about. First of all I offered Merle (the gate-crasher!) a prehistoric bird-thing called *Dimorphodon*—did I tell you I only know the names because they were on the costumes? It's a *pterosaur*. One thing this business has done is improve my education, but that's the best anyone can say about it, as you'll know when you read the papers.

Anyway, *Dimorphodon* has great, leather-looking wings and Merle said the costume would make her look like a bat out of hell, for it has the most repulsive head half as long as its body and hideous, overlapping teeth. She made such a fuss that I gave it—the two of them, rather—to Pippa and Jennifer, who were quite pleased, actually. It was like Merle's cheek to beef about what she was offered, anyway.

You and I had *Saltoposuchas,* which I thought, with all that iridescent blue and green colouring and the splashes of red-brown, was quite the prettiest costume of the lot, and Polly and Sophie had *Diatryma,* which reminded me of the sort of ostrich you could only see in a nightmare. Polly said it was indecent because they had to straddle their legs so much that they were reduced (I must admit) to a rather obscene waddling when they had to move about.

Anyway, as my little brother had seized one of the two *iguanodon* costumes, I thought Merle could have the other. She wasn't very gracious about that, either, and did not join in the charades. It seemed she had a chip on her shoulder all evening, I thought, knowing that it was her brother I'd invited, but the wretch sent her instead. I'd have had the charades *before* the dancing, so that people could take the costumes off and have a long, cool drink (I didn't think much of my grandmother's claret-cup, did you?) before beginning the dancing, but there was a reason for the reversal. The consequence was that when people had danced and then were told to dress up, I don't think the majority were any too keen. The costumes were hot and some of them were heavy and the charades we could do in them were so very limited that I think we were all glad when both sides had done one little sketch and we could all opt out of doing another.

At this point, of course, the thing would have been to get rid of the costumes, settle for supper and a bit of relaxation and then go on with the dancing. Well, Maisy, this is where I blame myself. I wanted a special memento of my birthday, so I'd arranged for a professional photographer (at my grandmother's expense, I'm afraid) to come at about eleven and photograph the lot of us in our fancy dress and then, later on, with us in our party frocks. He was also to take family groups, groups of friends, me with my presents, and so on. That's why I put the dancing first. I couldn't have the photographer come earlier because he had an engagement to take photographs at a banquet in the town.

So at the end of the charades people were still hanging about in those wretched costumes waiting for thc photographer and going out on to the terrace to cool off and that's when Merle did her disappearing act. She announced that she was going to stroll a little way down the drive. I said, 'Not at this time of night?' She said, 'Why not? I shan't meet anybody, and if I did I should only scare them into a decline, dressed like this. You're a nuisance to make us keep the things on.'

She was always a bit of an ass, as you know from our schooldays, and I believe she half-hoped she *would* meet somebody, but whether by accident (which was what she indicated) or by design (which is what *I* suspect) I suppose we shall never know unless something comes out at the inquest. Anyway, she was in a peculiar mood all along and never turned up for the photographs at all, but, actually, neither did the photographer!

Well, I don't want to run her down, but, in spite of what the papers will say, she was a bitch and a schemer, as well as being an ass. Still, *absit invidia* and all that.

You know what I'm trying to tell you, don't you, Maisy? She *did* meet someone and whoever it was must have given her a fearful bashing. When daddy and Nigel and my angel doctor-boy went out to look for her, she was dead. The *iguanadon* head she'd been wearing was no thicker on top than a cotton skull-cap and the police think she was bashed on the head first and then the costume was dragged off her, because they found it ripped to bits and scattered around the body.

Lionel's Letter

These hols. have been pretty dim up to now, Monkey, but they have taken a turn for the better and that's why I'm writting except to say arent you glad we are haveing Mr Peters next term instead of old Scruffy although Mr Peters keeps a slipper hooked on to a nail at the side of the blackbord by the duster Tim Banks calls it Mr Peters secret weppon but I don't think Peters is vishous do you and coaches Rugger jolly well I hope

I get into the third XV bet I do so nerts to Goldberg who fancys himself at scrum half because he is Cohens cozzen and the Jews always stick together wish my family did grandma is beastly strict although really quite all right but my parents are mostly abroad and I don't see all that much of them although regular pocket-money which is the main thing I serpose.

New para as old Scruffy would say what a mean old ass still never mind him I must tell you about our murder they think I don't know but you can get to know everything if you sneek along to the kitchen door and lissen to the cook and the others in there.

New para well, my cocky sister had a party on her birthday with some jolly good costumes she wangled her friend he's a doctor and not bad has played for the Babas though only once he got her the costumes and I collared one it was an iguanadon I know how you spell it because it is labled.

New para well there was this party and this girl was the other iguanadon only Dr Tassel what a name I bet they ragged him at school calls it something else which I cant spell but it's still an iguanadon like an eider or a widgen or a mallard is still a duck if you see what I mean anyway this girl went out late at night to get cooled off I bet they had all been drinking a lot of shampane and sherry and stuff like that and she got murdered they will not let me go to the inquest so I have disided to become a detective and help the police find the murderer I bet they can do with some help don't you wish you were here there are two village kids I play with one is a girl but quite sensible so I may let them come in on the murder they very desently let me come in on their secret cottage its filthy but very interesting so I may let them be my asisternts in the murder as three would be better than one if the murderer turns nasty and they can both box.

New para Ive got to give back the costume but I don't care much because it would be too awkward to pack to take home and Amabel says it makes her feel sick to think its the same as the girl had on when she was murdered they won't let me see the body its in the mortchery which I think is like an ice-box to keep bodys fresh till the coroner has seen them I wouldnt mind being a coroner and seeing all the bodys but I'd rather be a detective because thats where the action is and you look for cloos and measure footprints and pick up cigarette ends not to smoke but to notiss the brand and deduce things like whether a man is left-handed or limps and all that see you on the 23rd bring another of those jam sponges I think I can sneek too tins of sardeens Tim Banks can come in with us if he brings anything desent baked beans would do but a tin of cooked ham would be better.

P.S. They have just told me we're all going home the police have got our address so will let us go how rotten I would much rather stay here.

A Godfather's Letter

I would be shocked and horrified by the flippant tone of your recent communication, my dear boy, if I did not realise that you have been through a trying and a traumatic experience which must have left you disturbed and perhaps conscience-stricken over the death of that poor young girl whom (let us not mince matters) you jilted.

However, some parts of your letter appear to require an answer, so I will state at once that I have no intention of intruding on Mrs Kempson. There is nothing I can do to help her through this very difficult and harassing time. Neither shall I attend the inquest on poor little Merle Patterson to hear you give your contribution to the evidence.

As for Amabel Kempson-Conyers, I regard her as a spoilt brat and I doubt very much whether you have the strength of character to cope with her. I send you my regards, although I doubt whether you deserve them. Come and see me at Christmas, as usual.

CHAPTER 10

The Hermit's Cottage

Kenneth and I decided, I remember, that our real adventures began when Aunt Kirstie told us that we need not go to the village school on Monday, as it was uncertain how long our mother would remain in hospital and so we might be sent for at any moment to return home. We endorsed this point of view.

'There wouldn't be much sense in our signing on just for a week, perhaps,' said Kenneth. 'Only muck up the teacher's register.'

'What happens if the attendance officer comes round?' I remember asking. In our London school the attendance officer was a familiar figure, a short, thick-set, po-faced young man in a blue serge suit and a burberry who looked at the registers and took down the names and addresses of absentees. Then he went to their homes to find out whether they were ill or whether they were playing the wag or whether, if girls, they were being kept away from school to help with the housework, or whether, if boys, they had no boots or were running errands for tradesmen. In our day the attendance officer was a feared and detested figure in all the poorer parts of the town.

'Attendance officer? Who's he?' Uncle Arthur enquired. 'Only body likely to enquire about you is the governess, because they're paid according to numbers on roll.'

Monday passed pleasantly. The weather was fine, we were free, we found three golf-balls on that part of The Marsh which was the University golf-course, we paddled, fished for tiddlers, picked and ate grandfather's fruit and paid a visit to the hermit's stinking cottage to look at Mr Ward's filled-in hole.

The one place we felt we must not visit was the sheepwash. We had been put on our honour not to go near it, so when Our Ern and a bigger boy suggested a visit to it, we said we were compelled to refuse.

'Aw, come on, then!' they said.

'Can't. We've promised not to.'

'Aw, come on!'

'No, not this time.'

'Dare ee!'

'No good. No dare taken.'

'Checken-'earted, then!'

'If you say that again,' said Kenneth, 'the next time we go bathing down by Long Bridges I shall drown you.'

Long Bridges was about two miles from the village. It was a back-water of the river around part of which the town council had put corrugated iron fencing and had built dressing-sheds. There were stone steps slippery with weed leading down to the water. As a treat we were allowed to go there in charge of a village girl who came in once a week to help Aunt Kirstie turn out Mr Ward's rooms and who received an extra sixpence for taking us to the bathing-place.

Unlike Lionel at his private school, we were compelled in so public a place to wear bathing costumes. These had been fabricated for us by Aunt Kirstie out of one of her voluminous red flannel petticoats.

'Ought to be blue stockinette,' said Uncle Arthur, and how heartily we agreed with him!

'Flannel will keep them warm in the water,' said Aunt Kirstie. 'I don't want them catching their deaths.'

Kenneth's threat to drown Our Ern was met by a far more formidable counter-threat.

'Ef ee don't come down the sheepwash Oi'll tell Gov'ness you ent attenden school. Your auntie and uncle'll go to preson ef you ent attenden school.'

So we forfeited our honour and went along to the sheep-wash, deeming it better to feel besmirched than to risk putting Uncle Arthur and Aunt Kirstie in gaol.

''Tes 'ereabouts as her bled,' said Our Ern ghoulishly. We searched diligently for bloodstains, but did not find any.

'Anyways, they've got 'em as done et,' Our Ern went on.

'Garn!' said the big boy. 'They never!'

'Tell ee they 'ave, then. They've tooken that geppo what go weth Old Sukie. Our Sarah said so. Strong as a loyon he be, and took four p'licemen to get hem ento the Black Maria.'

'Oi warnts moi tea,' said the boy, abandoning the argument. On the way back we saw Uncle Arthur coming home from work across The Marsh. He had whitewash on his clothes and carried his bag of tools. We waited for him. Kenneth took the bag and I held on to Uncle Arthur's arm.

'No good you canoodling round me,' he said, not attempting, however, to disengage himself. 'You been down the sheepwash, I'll lay.'

'We couldn't help it,' I said, 'and we're going to tell Aunt Kirstie. Is it true the police have arrested one of the gypsies? Is it Old Sukie's man?'

'So I heard tell.'

'But they can't do that,' said Kenneth. 'The murder happened at night, didn't it?'

'What do *you* know about it?'

'It's all over the village. Everybody knows. The thing is, you see, the gypsy couldn't have done it.'

'Oh?' We crossed the plank bridge. I had been the one to open the iron gate. I stayed to close it. Kenneth, who had been tagging along behind with the bag of tools, caught up with Uncle Arthur.

'Of course he couldn't,' he said. 'Don't you remember? He was at the fair. Why should they think he did it? Didn't he tell them where he was? And didn't Sukie back him up? She was there, too, you know. She tried to fight those beasts who set on him.'

'Oh, nobody don't pay no attention to what them gyppos

says,' said Uncle Arthur. 'Liars and thieves, every man jack of 'em.'

'But if the police think he's a murderer they might hang him,' I said. (Hanging was then the punishment for murder.)

'Good riddance to bad rubbish,' said Uncle Arthur. 'Ten to one, if it wasn't him it was another of 'em. They're all alike.'

But we could not leave it at that. We talked matters over and then decided to go next day to see Mrs Kempson. This time we went to the front door. When the butler opened it and saw us, he said,

'Master Lionel has gone home.'

'We know,' said Kenneth. 'Miss Margaret and Mr Kenneth Clifton, to see Mrs Kempson on business.' He handed the butler his cap. 'It's to do with the murder,' he said. The butler stood aside and let us in.

'Very good, sir,' he said ironically. 'But may I point out that it is customary for gentlemen to 'and me their 'ats *after* they have crossed the threshold? This way, if you please.'

He did not take us up the splendid staircase, but led the way to a small, pretty little room on the ground floor.

'Miss Margaret Clifton, Mr Kenneth Clifton,' he announced. It ought to have sounded all right and, in a way, it *did* sound all right, but we knew he was laughing at us.

'Oh, I'm afraid Lionel has gone home,' said Mrs Kempson. Seated in the room with her was a small, thin lady, not so old as Mrs Kempson. She had black hair and black eyes and her hands and face looked rather yellow. She was so much like a witch that I ought to have been alarmed, but (as Kenneth said later) somehow you knew she was all right.

I thought it was about time that I said something. So far, I had left all the talking to Kenneth.

'We know Lionel has gone home. He told us,' I said. 'We've come about the murder.'

'Good gracious me! What do you children know about that?'

'We know the gypsy didn't do it.'

'How can you know anything of the sort?' But, as she asked the question, she turned to the black-haired lady. 'I think perhaps I had better leave this to you, Mrs Bradley. I don't know what these children are talking about,' she said.

'Interesting,' said Mrs Bradley. 'Oh, are you leaving us?'

'Yes, I have letters to write.' Somewhat to our relief, Mrs Kempson got up to go. She told us to sit down and then she left us with the black-haired witch. She walked out very slowly, as though she was weak and ill.

'The inquest is tomorrow,' said Mrs Bradley, fixing her sharp eyes on us. 'This will be the preliminary enquiry, you know, when the body is formally identified and the medical evidence taken, so you have come at a very good time. Forgive me if it is an impertinent question, but are not the school holidays over?'

'We don't really belong here,' said Kenneth. 'We expect to go back to London any day now.'

'I see. And what did you want to tell Mrs Kempson?'

'It wasn't so much Mrs Kempson,' I explained. 'It's just that we had to tell somebody important, and she's the only important person we know except our grandfather, and I don't think he'd be interested.'

'Oh, and why is that?'

'He doesn't like gypsies. He says they raid his chicken-run and I think perhaps they do.'

'I see. Suppose you begin at the beginning. I feel that your story will be fraught with interest.'

I wondered whether she also was laughing at us. In what turned out to be a long acquaintance with her, for we were among the first to congratulate her when, many years later, she was made a D.B.E. and had to be addressed (rather to our embarrassment) as Dame Beatrice, we never really did know when she was laughing at us, but she was so good to us—helping us to get good jobs and rooting for Kenneth to get him into Parliament later on—that we did not mind even if she *was* indulging her unpredictable sense of humour at our expense, for it was puzzling but never hurtful.

Anyway, before we left Mrs Kempson's house that day we had laid all before her and she had promised to see that Sukie's man got justice. I do not know, even to this day, what gave us such complete confidence in her, but she came to see

Uncle Arthur and he agreed to give Bellamy Smith a complete alibi, as was only just and right.

'Well,' said Kenneth, when we were on our way back to Aunt Kirstie's. 'I think we can depend on her, don't you? She seems a very reliable sort of person. She talked to us as if we were grown-up and she didn't ask any silly questions.'

'There's an awful lot of the day left. What shall we do after dinner?' I asked.

'I know what I *want* to do, but I don't know whether you'll agree, and it's not a job I want to tackle on my own.'

'You mean the hermit's cottage, don't you? I don't want to go there again.'

'I thought you wouldn't, but remember that filled-in hole!'

'What about it?'

'I rather *think*,' said Kenneth, kicking a stone in front of him as we walked down the hill, 'I *rather* think Mr Ward may have buried something there, you know.'

'Why? What makes you think so?' I no longer thought of buried treasure. I had murder in mind and I was frightened.

'Well, why should he dig a hole like that and then fill it in again if he wasn't burying something?' said Kenneth. 'He'd never do all that work for nothing. Nobody would.'

'He might if he was a madman.'

'They think a madman murdered that girl, and *we* think Mr Ward is a bit mad. Tell you what! Suppose there's some important clue to him being the murderer and he's buried it in that cottage so the police won't find it? Wouldn't it be a score if we dug it up and it turned out to be just the thing the police were looking for? It *could* be, you know, because I don't suppose they realise Mr Ward used to go to the cottage and dig up the floor.'

Aunt Kirstie hardly ever asked what we had been doing with ourselves during the morning or what we were going to do after dinner and she did not do so on this occasion. We slipped out while she was doing the washing-up and went down to the duckpond. Grandfather, we knew, would be settling down for his afternoon nap and Aunt Lally would be doing her own washing-up, so the coast was clear. All the same, we went a long way round to get to the gap we had made in the hermit's iron railings. We took cover among raspberry canes and currant bushes after we had skirted the duckpond, then we went behind the pigsties and, having reached old Polly's stable, we took cover behind that and waited and listened. I still did not want to go to the cottage, but I was afraid of Kenneth's going alone.

There was nobody about, so we made for the gap in the fence and squeezed through. Unless somebody looked over the side wall which had glass on top to keep children from climbing in, we knew we could not be spotted, for the people who lived next door had put up a very high fence between them and the hermit's untidy garden. We tip-toed up what was left of the garden path, listened at the back doorway and then went in through the kitchen to the front room.

There was the filled-in hole and near it lay Mr Ward's pickaxe. It was then that Kenneth said, 'Well, that's no use to us. We ought to have brought a spade.'

'That wouldn't be much use, either,' I said. 'We tried Uncle Arthur's once, don't you remember? We couldn't do much with it, even in his garden. I vote we chuck this and find something else to do.'

'And leave the treasure, or maybe the clue to the murder?'

'Well, what's the use? We can't get it on our own. Besides . . .'

'Besides what?'

'We might find there wasn't any treasure or any clue and then we, or whoever helped us, would have had all the sweat for nothing.' (I did not express my real fear of what we might find.)

'Oh, rot! If Mr Ward filled in the hole, he *must* have buried something. Stands to reason.'

'Not if he's mad it doesn't,' I said again.

'You said "whoever helped us". I've thought of somebody who would.'

'They're all in school, and, anyway, it wouldn't be our secret any longer.'

'Poachy Ling isn't in school.'

'But he's barmy.'

'All the better. He won't know what it's all about, and he's as strong as a horse. He's always hanging about and trying to join in things. He'd come like a shot if we asked him.'

'He gibbers and dribbles. I'm scared of him.'

'He's all right. Just a bit simple, Uncle Arthur says. That's why he doesn't go to proper work. Does odd jobs here and there and helps his mother with her washing. Let's go and see if he's hanging about anywhere.'

Poachy Ling was usually to be found hanging about. He was called Poachy not because he had a talent for snaring rabbits or taking pheasants, but because it was the nearest he ever got to pronouncing his own name, which was Percy. He was known to be harmless, but his moppings and mowings always made me uneasy and anxious to get away from him. In other words he was the village idiot, but an older brother protected him and Our Sarah would not permit any of her gang to tease him when his brother was at work. Neither, however, would she have him as a member of her group, although he was always, in a hopeful spirit, trying to become a camp-follower. I suppose he must have had the mentality of a retarded child of four. I believe his age in years was twenty-three.

'Even if we had Poachy we still haven't got a spade,' I said.

'There's Uncle Arthur's in the shed. You go and get that, and I'll go and find Poachy.'

'Uncle Arthur might be waxy.'

'Not he. He let us dig in the garden with it.'

Digging in Uncle Arthur's garden and digging up the floor of the hermit's filthy hovel seemed to my mind two very different things, but I did not say so. I sneaked back to Aunt Kirstie's while Kenneth went out by the front door of the cottage. Luckily the shed was at the bottom of the garden next to the earth closet, so I did not need to go near the house. I secured the heavier of Uncle Arthur's two spades, added the iron crowbar we had borrowed when we forced the palings apart, and returned to the garden of the cottage.

I waited there for what seemed a very long time before

Kenneth re-appeared. He came back through the cottage and found me poking about among the bushes with the crowbar.

'What are you doing?' he asked.

'Nothing. I've found something, though. Show you later. Where's Poachy?'

'In the road. Come and help me make him come in.' He picked up the spade, I followed with the crowbar and we dumped them on top of the filled-in hole. Poachy was writhing about and talking to himself. I took one arm and Kenneth took the other and we persuaded him into the cottage. Kenneth showed him the spade, handed it to him and indicated the place where we wanted him to dig. I picked up the crowbar and retreated towards the kitchen. I think I had some vague idea of protecting Kenneth in case Poachy turned nasty—not that he ever did.

Apparently the suggestion conveyed by the spade and the newly tramped-down earth appealed to something in the idiot's memory. He fell into a series of weird contortions, grinned and slobbered, picked up the spade and fell to work. Soon earth and stones were flying in all directions, so Kenneth and I took cover in the kitchen doorway, peeping out every now and again to see how he was getting on.

'What *were* you poking in the bushes for?' Kenneth asked, while Poachy delved and heaved. 'You said you found something. What?'

'A boot,' I said, 'elastic-sided. I believe it's one of Mr Ward's.'

CHAPTER 11

Our Special Correspondent

With no desire or intention of being facetious, for, in the circumstances we are about to describe, such an attitude on the part of this newspaper would be in the worst possible taste, we have to admit that, if the horror films want it, Hill village has it. Figure to yourself, as the French are supposed to say, two murders, each as bizarre as the other, in a village of under three hundred inhabitants and within a space of less than three weeks! Does your mind boggle? Not half as much as the mind of the local inspector of police, we dare swear!

Our readers will remember—indeed, who, knowing the facts, could ever forget?—the death of Miss Merle Patterson, a stranger from London who was found brutally done to death at the end of a grassy thoroughfare known locally as Lovers' Lane.

Miss Patterson, it will be recalled, had strayed away from a party held at Hill Manor House, just outside the now notorious and fateful village of Hill, and was found battered and bathed in blood at round about three o'clock in the morning.

Her cruel death was and remains a mystery. It is clear that Hill village must house an undetected homicidal maniac. He has now claimed another victim in the person of a quiet, inoffensive, elderly man said to have been related to the chatelaine of Hill Manor, Mrs Emilia Kempson, the Great Lady of the village and the hostess at what has become known as the fateful birthday party.

The facts relating to this second apparently motiveless murder are obscure. For two nights Mr Ward had not slept in his bed or returned to his lodgings for his supper. Interviewed by us, his landlady, Mrs Christine (Kirstie) Landgrave, told us:

'Mr Ward was not the sort to make enemies. Whoever killed him must be a madman. I do not know any more about Mr Ward than what Mrs Kempson told me, which was that he had lived many years in Canada and the States and had come back to England to find work, but was too old, she thought, to fend for himself and as he was a distant relative—that is how she described him—she was prepared to pay me to look after him and would provide him with his bit of spending money.

'That is all I know about Mr Ward. He was not one to talk about himself. If you got as much as a good morning from him it was quite a surprise. I had a terrible shock when I heard he was dead, especially when I heard where he was buried. I did not want to go to the mortuary, but my husband lost half a day's work to come with me and Mrs Kempson made that up to us, seeing that, if we had not gone, it would have had to be her, I suppose.

'Yes, I have my sister's children staying with me. No, I won't let you talk to them. They can't tell you anything you don't know, and the police have questioned them already and more than once. It is true they were at the cottage where the body was found. No, I don't suppose you can get much sense out of poor Poachy, but I won't allow Maggie and Ken to be questioned again and I shall tell the police if you try. No, I don't want your money. The children knew there had been a hole dug in the floor of that cottage, though why they wanted to go and play in such a dirty, tumbledown old place, when they'd got so many other places to play in, I don't know, but that's children, isn't it?

'No, I have never seen the young lady that was murdered down at the sheepwash, but it must have been the same man as killed Mr Ward, mustn't it? It stands to reason. You couldn't have two murderers in a village this size.

'Oh, yes, the children are going home as soon as their father can come down here to fetch them. No, they haven't had a shock. They never stayed to see Poachy actually dig up the body, you see. They come running back as soon as they saw a bit of Mr Ward's suit and one of his hands. He had a signet ring with a big stone in it and you couldn't mistake his clothes. The coat was a sort of a dirty mustard colour. Nobody else in the village has one like it, and the children recognised that and they found one of his boots in the garden.'

So much for Mrs Landgrave. We respected her wishes concerning the children, but we have made other enquiries among the inhabitants of Hill, although the veil of mystery surrounding the two apparently motiveless murders seems to be impenetrable. We may add that although they do not admit outright to holding a council of despair—we put it like that because we hear that Scotland Yard will have to be involved sooner or later and we would suggest that preferably it ought to be sooner—there is no doubt that at present the local police are completely baffled.

This appears to be a classic case of a murderer whose lust for killing may be disguised under an exterior as bland and innocent as yours or mine, dear reader. He may be a Neill Cream or a Jack the Ripper, planning already where he will strike again. That possibility cannot be ruled out. This maniac must be apprehended and that right speedily.

The police are attempting to find some connexion between the two deaths, but there appear to be very few points of resemblance. Consider the known facts. Here we tabulate them side by side for purposes of comparison.

1. A girl aged twenty.	1. A man of late middle age.
2. Gently nurtured.	2. Possibly a rough diamond.
3. A loving family and plenty of friends.	3. One known relative who sends him to lodge with strangers and never sees him again, not even after his death. (We do not intend any criticism. There must have been good reasons.)

4. Murdered after leaving a birthday party, ostensibly to go out for a breath of air.	4. Murdered after having been absent from his lodgings for no known reason.
5. Wearing fancy dress which could have acted as a disguise.	5. Wearing clothes which were readily identifiable by anyone in the village.
6. Came from London and knew nobody in the village except the persons present at the party.	6. Came from America, but known by sight to everybody in the village.
7. Sociable and lively.	7. Unsociable and non-communicative.
8. Body left by sheepwash although probably killed nearer Hill House.	8. Body buried in hole he himself had dug, probably from boredom with his uneventful existence.
9. Head smashed in. Fancy dress torn off.	9. Head smashed in. Boots taken off.
10. Found by search-party sent to look for her.	10. Found by accident.
11. Gypsies suspected but cleared.	11. No obvious suspects, certainly not gypsies who never passed cottage en route to sell or beg in town.
12. Children accustomed to play down by sheepwash.	12. Children known to have played in ruined cottage.

13. Killed at approx. eleven p.m. on the Saturday. Body found at three a.m. on following morning.	13. Killed possibly on the Friday. Body found some days later.
14. Connected with Hill House (festivities).	14. Connected with Hill House (relationship).

And so, for the time being, the matter rests. It has to be borne in mind that whereas Mr Ward's death could have been premeditated—there is a theory that he may have been slaughtered somewhere else and taken to the cottage for burial—it hardly seems likely that Miss Patterson's murder was previously planned. Readers will remember that she had not been invited to Hill House, but was taking her brother's place. Did the murderer—since she was wearing a bulky and not very attractive fancy dress—mistake her for her brother?

We think the police might give this point more serious consideration than, so far, they appear to have done. To our mind this matter needs far more probing into than it has yet received.

Hill Manor House

The manor itself is mentioned in Domesday Book and seems to have been of moderate wealth. The entry, part of which, by courtesy of Professor Donald Cuttie who translated the abbreviations for us, we reproduce, states that 'William de Gyffe holds Hill. It was always assessed for forty hides. The land is twenty-five carucates. In the demesne there are three hides and a half. There are two ploughs there. Among the free men and the villeins there are fifteen ploughs and five more could be made.'

And so on and so forth. The entry goes on to list the tenants' various holdings, mentions the fact that the manor had a mill—some distance from the present village if it was a water-mill, we would think!—and notes that the value of the property had dropped since it was valued in the reign of Edward the

Confessor, although how that value was arrived at seems to be speculative.

The historians tell us no more of Hill until the reign of Queen Elizabeth I, when the property came into the hands of a wealthy clothier from Somerset, who built the present Hill Manor House. It is a moderate-sized mansion erected in pleasant, mellow, Cotswold stone. It came into the hands of Mrs Kempson's grandfather by purchase towards the end of last century. The original gatehouse fell into disrepair and was demolished in 1906 to make way for a lodge which, owing to the shortage of domestic staff, is now untenanted, and past which it seems probable that Miss Patterson strayed on the night of her death.

The main feature of the mansion is a magnificent oak staircase leading up to the principal rooms. These rooms themselves, with their decorated plaster ceilings and Tudor fireplaces, are, we understand, show pieces. It was in the largest and grandest of these rooms, known as the *grand salon,* that the ill-fated young and attractive Merle Patterson was disporting herself shortly before her tragic and horrible death.

There is no legend of the customary 'grey lady' who haunts so many sixteenth- and seventeenth-century manor houses, but if we were inclined to superstition (and who is not?) we might be forgiven if we fancied we met a 'glimmering girl', as W. B. Yeats expresses it, flitting about the grounds of Hill Manor House. The police have not yet decided exactly where Merle Patterson and Mr Ward were actually done to death (it now seems unlikely that these spots were Lovers' Lane and the cottage), or what sudden panic caused the murderer to throw what seems to have been his bloody (we use the word in its Shakespearian sense—i.e. 'What bloody man is that?' *Macbeth,* Act 1 Sc. 2) his bloody weapon into the sheep-wash.

Did someone who has not come forward, but who could be, perhaps, the only person on earth who could help the police with their enquiries, did someone actually surprise the murderer just as he had concluded one or other of his devilish machinations? If so, we would remind this person of his civic duties and beg him to be manly and courageous enough to come forward and tell what he knows.

If there is such a man (or woman, for the matter of that) he is assured of complete police protection from the instant he decides to open his mouth. The murderer has struck twice. It should be a matter of conscience to someone, somewhere, to come forward and help to make sure that he does not strike again.

Post Scriptum

Your correspondent has just heard that after diligent and patient search for clues, the police have come to the conclusion that Miss Patterson was enticed or forced into the disused lodge at Hill Manor House and done to death there. The public, needless to say, are rigidly excluded from the grounds.

Part Two: Verdict

CHAPTER 12

Mrs Lestrange Bradley Takes a Hand

Well might I say with the Apostle, 'The former treatise have I made, O Theophilus,' for I have kept you informed to some extent, my dear Sir Walter, of what has been happening during the past weeks at the Oxfordshire village of Hill. However, it now seems possible and desirable to furnish you with a fuller and more connected narrative of events, if only to clarify my own mind by airing my theories concerning their import.

As you know, I was called to Hill Manor House in my professional capacity by Mrs Kempson, in order to examine and report upon the mental state of a man who claimed to be her brother. As you also know, she then cancelled the appointment on the score of his disappearance.

Well, he has turned up again, not quick but dead. His body has been dug up from the floor of a derelict cottage by the village idiot. As though the murder of Merle Patterson, whose body, you will remember, was found near the sheepwash at the end of the village, were not sufficiently mysterious, we now have this bizarre occurrence to add to the tally.

The inquest on Miss Patterson resulted in a verdict of murder by person or persons unknown, although the police, acting somewhat precipitately, had arrested a gypsy named Bellamy Smith for the crime. They were obliged to release him, however, as, thanks to two intelligent young children and their uncle, Bellamy was able to prove a complete alibi. The contention of the police that he had suffered a torn ear in his struggle with the girl was shown to be mistaken. His earring had been dragged out during a scuffle with some drunken louts in a wrestling booth at the annual fair.

There has been considerable speculation as to what the girl was doing down at the sheepwash at all so late at night, and still in her fancy dress, but, since the release of the gypsy, the police believe that she was not killed where she was found. They think she was murdered very much nearer the manor house, probably inside a deserted lodge in the grounds, and are busily searching for any clues which will prove this. It is a tenable hypothesis and seems to fit in with the facts so far as we know them, but they are merely skeletal and inconclusive.

Whether the two murders are connected in any way seems doubtful. The police are inclined to think that we have a homicidal maniac roaming the neighbourhood and Mrs Kempson, who has called me in again more, I think, to bear her company in that big old house than for any other reason, inclines to the same view and has despatched her young grandson, his sister and their parents to their London flat to be out of harm's way. Her adopted son is also in London, where, I understand, he has employment, so she really is very lonely and I suspect apprehensive too.

The whole case bristles with difficulties. To begin with, there seems little doubt that Mr Ward was, to say the least, an eccentric. According to the respectable people with whom, at Mrs Kempson's expense, he lodged, he was a silent, ruminative man who gave no trouble but who was strangely uncommunicative. The first indication they had of his mental derangement was when he began by digging up one of their flower-beds, passed on to a large chicken-run and dug that up, then began operations on the boardless floor of the tumbledown cottage where somebody (most probably his murderer, but this has not been established) later buried his body.

The people with whom he lodged are named Christina (Kirstie) and Arthur Landgrave, and they have staying with them the two intelligent young children I mentioned. These are aged ten and eight and from them I have derived some of my information. Having watched Mr Ward's operations on the flower-bed and in the chicken-run, they also saw him come out from the ruined cottage, where he had begun to dig a hole, and later they observed him standing in the sheep-wash wielding a pickaxe. Later still, they discovered that he had considerably enlarged the hole in the cottage floor so that it resembled a grave. As we now know, this resemblance became apparent to somebody other than the children.

To revert to Mr Ward, until his body was discovered, the police, guided by a statement from Mrs Kempson after the gypsy had been released from custody, thought that Mr Ward might have killed the girl, particularly as a spade believed to be his was found at the bottom of the sheepwash. According to Mrs Kempson, she had received complaints from the Landgraves concerning his strange behaviour and had no difficulty in believing that he could have become homicidal.

The trouble about this supposition is that the medical evidence is not conclusive as to whether the girl or Ward died first. You probably know how impossible it can be to become dogmatic in such matters when the time limits can fall within a matter of hours and when one body has been in the open air for a comparatively short time, whereas the other has been buried for several days before being found.

Besides, if Ward killed the girl and then committed suicide in a most unlikely manner, who buried him? Otherwise, who killed both of them, and why? Further to that, are the police looking for two murderers in a small village which is built on only two streets? It seems unlikely.

I will tell you what else I have found out so far, although you will appreciate that, as the newspapers say of the police, I am still pursuing my enquiries. Before I go on I must add that the police have uncovered no motive for either death which seems capable of bearing closer examination. Mr Ward appears to have given up all claim to the Hill Manor estate, which is now entailed on Mrs Kempson's grandson, a boy of nine named Lionel Kempson-Conyers, and as for Merle Patterson, she appears to have known nobody in the village except the people who attended the birthday party.

In any case, it seems that she was present without having received a card of invitation, but was acting as stand-in for her brother, so it hardly looks as though her death could have been premeditated, neither can anybody trace the slightest connexion between her death and that of Mr Ward except that the same murder weapon may have been used for both. The police have taken possession of a heavy garden spade which they believe was the implement employed.

One point of interest which has emerged is that the dead girl, at her own request, had changed costumes at the party with young Lionel Kempson-Conyers, but whether the fact has any bearing on her death has yet to be discovered. I have the assurance from Doctor Tassall, who was present when Merle's body was found and who was the negotiating agency between the medical students who had fabricated the costumes and their subsequent purchase by the Kempson family, that, except for size and a very slight variation in colouring, the exchanged costumes were exactly alike, so this may have some significance, but only if somebody was anxious to get Lionel out of the way by killing him.

This seems to eliminate Ward from our list of suspects even if he were not dead, since he had told Mrs Kempson that although he had inherited the estate, he could not afford to keep it up and pay the servants, and Mrs Kempson has confirmed this by telling me that it is only because of the fortune left her by her late husband that she herself can afford to go on living at Hill House. Incidentally, she tells me that she was leaving Ward a compensatory sum in her will.

Well, we are left with a most unsatisfactory list of suspects for the murder of Miss Patterson and no suspects whatever for the death of Ward unless (so far as I can see at present) he was an eye-witness when the girl was killed and so was children and, perhaps, their playmates, knew that the hole himself had made in the cottage floor But who, except the children and, perhaps, their playmates, knew that the hole in the floor so conveniently existed? That, I think, is a most interesting and important point.

I ought to add that Ward, on Mr and Mrs Landgraves'

evidence, had not slept at his lodgings for two nights, so the hypothesis that he was a witness of Miss Patterson's murder is hardly tenable, for my own theory is that he was already dead when she was killed, although, of course, he may have murdered her and been slaughtered by somebody out of revenge. My contention at present is that Miss Patterson was mistaken for young Lionel, but then we are faced with a key question. Failing Mr Ward, who had already repudiated his inheritance, to whose advantage would it be to have Lionel out of the way?—and, in any case who would expect a child to be in the open so late at night?

As for the opportunity to murder Merle Patterson, well, Doctor Tassall and the adopted son—I call him 'adopted' for convenience' sake—are known to have been out of the house at the time of the girl's murder. Mrs Kempson had gone to bed (her personal maid vouches for this) but, so far as I can tell, there was no reason why she should not have slipped out of her room between ten and eleven, left the house secretly and returned to it unnoticed while the party was in full swing. As for Lionel's parents, Mr and Mrs Conyers, they say they retired to their own quarters to escape the sounds of revelry. They certainly left the party, but there seems no confirmation of where they went. However, as they were hardly likely to desire the death of their only son, if either or both are murderers they must have intended to make Miss Patterson their victim. The question here is—why? They were acquainted with her, no doubt, since she and her brother belonged to their daughter's set in London and the girls had been at school together. However, I do not suspect Mrs Kempson or the Conyers of having any hand in the murders at all. Nigel Kempson and Doctor Tassall are the horses for my money.

CHAPTER 13

The Children's Crusade

It was at Kenneth's suggestion that we mobilised our forces in order to track down the murderer.

'Our Sarah,' he said, 'has always been decent, letting us join her gang and telling fibs for us and not splitting that time I uppercut Our Ern and landed him in the brook, so I reckon we ought to let her join in if she wants to. Besides, I expect she knows far more about the village than we do.'

'There's another thing, too,' I said. 'Safety in numbers.'

'How do you mean?'

'Well, if the murderer gets to know we're on his track, he could kill two of us as easy as wink. He might think twice about killing the whole of Our Sarah's gang, though.'

'It's a good point. Let's see what she says.'

Of course there had been terrific excitement when Poachy found what was buried in the hermit's cottage. As soon as we realised what it was, we begged him to stop digging, but he had worked himself up into a frenzy and went on stabbing away with the heavy spade, so, as we did not want to see any more than we had to see, although we knew for certain that it was Mr Ward, we rushed off home to get away from the grisly scene and dissociate ourselves from Poachy's findings if we could.

At least, that was my idea. We ran into the garden, but after we had squeezed through the gap in the iron railings and were on our way past Polly's stable, Kenneth stopped running and said,

'We'll have to tell them, you know. Somebody's got to stop Poachy. Besides, he might be blamed if we don't tell.'

Unfortunately Uncle Arthur was at work on a building site the other side of the town, and as we did not think the aunts would be much help in dealing with Poachy, that only left grandfather. We were afraid of him, but we felt that some man had to know, if only to stop Poachy from continuing his excavations.

Grandfather, I remember, was furious with us. Looking back, I realise that his anger was really horror to think that we should have mixed ourselves up with what obviously was a second case of murder.

When his diatribe (which was punctuated by threatening gestures with his walking-stick and with Aunt Lally's terrified exclamations and tearful reproaches) was over, he sent us to Aunt Kirstie with orders that she was to come immediately across to speak to him.

We found her feeding the ferrets. They belonged to Uncle Arthur and we were never allowed to handle them, but sometimes there would be rabbit pie or stewed rabbit with carrots, onions, turnips and small, fluffy dumplings for Sunday dinner instead of the usual pork or chicken.

Normally we enjoyed seeing the ferrets, but on this occasion there was no time for dallying. We did not want to tell Aunt Kirstie about our grim discovery in the derelict cottage, so we gave her grandfather's message and that was all.

'Oh, dear!' she said. 'Has he had one of his turns? I'd better get over as soon as I've changed my apron. Lally is that helpless she'll be crying and wringing her hands instead of doing something sensible about it.'

'I don't think he's ill,' I said, 'but he says to drop everything and come at once. I think he wants you to get on up to the big house. That's what he said.'

'To Mrs Kempson's? Whatever for? They haven't found poor Mr Ward, have they? That would be the only reason for me to go to Mrs Kempson's.'

'I think it *is* about Mr Ward,' I said.

'Must be,' she said. 'I'll be glad to have him back.' She bustled about, changed her clothes for what she called her 'decent bodice and skirt' and ran with us to the next-door house. Aunt Lally was indeed crying and wringing her hands, her usual reaction in times of crisis. Grandfather was sitting very upright and rigid in his armchair. He looked like Moses, I thought, or perhaps the prophet Jeremiah. His right hand was clutching the knob of his ebony, silver-topped stick and with his left fist he was banging the table.

Aunt Kirstie said, 'Well, father, is there something you want with me?'

Grandfather glared at her.

'Where's your lodger?' he demanded.

'I wish we knew, father. Hasn't slept in his bed since that Thursday night,' she said.

'Well, get you up to Mrs Kempson's, my girl, and tell her he's sound asleep now. Take this boy and girl with you. She'll want to know all the tale. And then keep them out of my sight for a bit. Bringing all this trouble on us!'

Aunt Kirstie stared at him.

'You mean as Mr Ward's dead?' she asked, dropping her voice at the last word.

'That's my meaning, my girl, or so it seems, so get on up there quick as you can. It isn't any business of ours, except these children of Elspeth's have seemingly dragged us into it. Don't stand there gaping at me! Get along! Get along!'

'I'll get my good coat and hat,' said Aunt Kirstie. 'Mr Ward dead! Oh, dear! Oh, dear! Whatever will Mrs Kempson have to say?'

'The children better have a clean-up, too, hadn't they, if you're going to the big house?' said Aunt Lally in an undertone, as she saw us out. Aunt Kirstie agreed. To get us washed and into our best clothes took a little time and when at last we started out, Aunt Kirstie said she could not hurry up the hill. However, we reached the manor house eventually and our aunt rang the bell.

Apparently it was the butler's afternoon off, for the door

was opened by a maidservant. Aunt Kirstie asked whether it would be convenient for her to speak to Mrs Kempson about something important, so, leaving us standing at the door, the maid said she would go and find out. She did not need to ask Aunt Kirstie's name. She came back in a very short time and took us to the ground-floor room in which Kenneth and I had been received the last time we had visited the manor house.

The room was in the sole possession of Mrs Bradley. She told us that Mrs Kempson was out, so, without consulting Aunt Kirstie, who did not know the whole truth, anyway, Kenneth told her our story. She listened without interrupting him. When, with a few interpolations from me and a few exclamations from Aunt Kirstie, he had finished the tale, she asked where the cottage was situated and then said she would ring up the police and that we had better return home at once, as the police would want to question us.

'Tell them the truth in a simple, orderly, straightforward fashion,' she said. 'Answer their questions briefly and to the point. I shall hope to see more of you later.' She told us to sit down while she telephoned. She had to go out of the room to do this, and while she was gone another maid brought Aunt Kirstie a cup of tea.

We could not tell the police much and I doubt whether they got anything at all useful from Poachy. Uncle Arthur was not very pleased when he came home.

'Police at my house?' he said. 'I've never been mixed up with the police, not the whole of my life. And where's it going to end? The law is cruel hard on poor people. It will be all right for that Kempson lot. They're rich. They'll get away with it. But he was our lodger, wasn't he? So they'll be on to us like the hand of God, and so I tell you, Kirstie.'

Aunt Kirstie harped upon another string.

'I don't know what come over you to want to go and play in that dirty old tumbledown shack,' she said sorrowfully. 'You got all our garden and all your grandfather's land, and the pigs and ducks and chickens and all, and your swing in the cartshed and all the fruit on the bushes, and The Marsh and the brook for your games. What call did you have to go and play in that there old dirty dump? Might have caught the fever or worse! And now we've lost our lodger, too, and not likely to get another when this comes out.'

We were silent. Her last observation affected us painfully, all the more so as it had not occurred to us, until she made it, that the death of Mr Ward, especially under such circumstances, would affect her and Uncle Arthur financially. Like my father and mother, they were anything but well off. Uncle Arthur's jobs on building sites—he was a plasterer by trade—were intermittent and I know now that, apart from allowing them to live rent-free—not nearly as much of a concession then as it would be nowadays—our grandfather, who disapproved of their marriage, did nothing to help them when they struck upon hard times, especially during the winter when there was no building going on. The most he would do—since he said once in my hearing that he could not let his daughter Kirstie starve—was to make the couple an occasional gift of a chicken or a piece of pork.

So we hung our heads and said nothing. The police came again next day, with more questions and with official notebooks in which they wrote down all Aunt Kirstie's answers about Mr Ward, and finished by saying that they would return in the evening when Uncle Arthur was home from work. We had taken refuge under the parlour table, which had a cover on it with a long fringe with bobbles on it. It formed an excellent hiding-place, and we heard the whole interview. Aunt Kirstie guessed we were there, I think, but perhaps she was glad of our company and moral support.

It was after the police had gone, and Aunt Kirstie had returned to the kitchen, and we had crawled out and sneaked down the back staircase into the scullery and the garden, that Kenneth said we must track down the murderer.

We had to wait until afternoon school came out before we could contact Our Sarah and her gang. By that time rumours of Poachy's horrid discovery were all over the village. The police had been seen going into Aunt Kirstie's house and it was known that two of them had dragged poor Poachy out of the hermit's cottage. Then his mother, who, alone of mankind, seemed able to interpret his gibberings, had gone into Miss Summers' shop to purchase a loaf of bread and spread the news. It was not known at that time who the dead man was, except to us and our family and Mrs Bradley. Even the police could not be dogmatic until the body had been formally identified, although their questioning of ourselves and Aunt Kirstie indicated their opinion clearly enough.

We did not intend to wait at the school gate for Our Sarah because we did not want to be spotted and identified by the governess as not having been at school, so we loitered outside the drill hall, knowing that Sarah and Ern would have to pass it on their way home.

We seemed to wait for a very long time, and Kenneth suggested that they must be playing on The Marsh. They hove in sight eventually and we went to meet them.

'Can't stop now,' said Our Sarah, before we could speak. 'Oi warnts moi tea.'

'After tea, then,' said Kenneth. 'It's fearfully important.'

Even Our Sarah, who had lofty ideas as to what was important and what was not, was compelled to allow our claim when we mentioned the cottage, later, after tea.

'Though Oi knows all about et,' she said, when we met at half-past five on The Marsh. 'Oi 'eard et en Mess Summers. That old nosey parker the Weddow Wenter was en there and her and Mess Summers was so busy yappen their selly 'eads orf as 'em never 'eard me come en. Tale dedn't lose nothen en the tellen, Oi'll be bound. Any road, take somethen special to breng the Weddow Wenter out from be'oind they aspedestriers of hern.'

'It was because of us that the body was discovered,' said Kenneth, repeating a phrase which the police inspector had used in our hearing when he was questioning Aunt Kirstie.

'Oi don't berlieve et.'

'It's true. We knew something was buried in that cottage, so we got Poachy to dig it up for us.'

'Then you be a body-snatcher, you young Oi say.'

'What's a body-snatcher?'

'Oi don't roightly know, but moi dad talk about 'em. Be

'anged for body-snatchen, ee can. They won't arf streng ee up 'oigh because you be only a lettle un and got no weight to ee, so they'll gev ee a long drop.'

'We didn't "snatch" anything. We simply found Mr Ward,' said Kenneth quickly.

'How do ee know as et was hem?'

'We saw a bit of that suit he always wore, and Margaret found one of his boots in the bushes. Look, Our Sarah, we want to find the murderer, because Mr Ward must have been murdered to have been buried like that. What we want to know is whether you and the gang will come in with us.'

'To look for a murderer? That's a p'lice job, that es.'

'Oh, please come in with us.'

'For whoi?'

'Well, to catch the murderer, like I said.'

'More loike the murderer 'ud ketch us, Oi reckon. Oi don't want no part of et.'

Kenneth gave up.

'It's no use arguing with her,' he said, as we made for the plank bridge and grandfather's iron gate. 'She won't budge. It's up to us, I reckon.'

Aunt Kirstie heard us come into the scullery. She told us not to make a noise because the police were interviewing Uncle Arthur upstairs in the parlour.

'And look you here,' she went on, 'I don't want you roaming about no more. You ain't to go on The Marsh or anywhere near that old cottage.'

'Police orders?' asked Kenneth.

'And mine and your grandfather's and your Uncle Arthur's. 'Tain't safe. I wishes as I could pack you both off home, but I can't do that till your father sends.'

We talked it over in the bedroom.

'What on earth shall we find to do?' I asked dolefully. 'Without the cottage—not that I really want to go there any more—and without The Marsh and the sheepwash, I don't see it's worth while being here any longer.'

'Of course it is,' said Kenneth. 'We're not forbidden the village streets and that's where we shall score. We've got to get at people and question them. Somebody must know something or have seen something. All we've got to do is find out what it is.'

'We can't just go knocking on doors.'

'I suppose not. Well, *you* think of something.'

As it happened, it was the Sunday school superintendent, and not myself, who thought of something, although he had no idea that he had solved the first part of our problem for us.

More or less incarcerated as we felt ourselves to be, even Sunday school seemed tolerable now that we had been deprived of our meetings on The Marsh with Our Sarah and her gang, so that when, on Sunday morning, Aunt Lally suggested it before she sent us over to get our breakfast from Aunt Kirstie, she found us in an unusually compliant mood.

We allowed ourselves without protest to be arrayed like the lilies of the field and set off in good time for the tin-roofed building. We settled ourselves in decorous silence, listened without comment to the young and ignorant teacher's exposition of the Sermon on the Mount and, when classes were over, paid attention to the superintendent's remarks before we had the closing hymn and his snuffling, unctuous, extempore closing prayer.

His little homily included the story of the Children's Crusade which took place in the Middle Ages. Then he urged us all to become Crusaders. (He did not mention that the unfortunate children never reached the Holy Land, but ended up in the slave markets of North Africa, and we did not know this at the time.) He drew a picture of their missionary zeal, their courage, their devotion to what he called The Cause and he finished up by saying that at the end of the meeting there would be collecting boxes for distribution to all those who would be willing to collect for Foreign Missions.

I looked across the room at the boys' side of the hall and caught Kenneth's eye. I made our tiny signal which meant *Shall we?* He nodded vigorously so, at the end of the session, we joined a small party of volunteers at the table where the star-cards were marked (an asterisk if you had attended and were punctual, a zero if you had attended but were late, the latter to count only half a mark towards the tally which meant a ticket for the Sunday school treat) and received our collector's card and a tin with a slit in the top.

The secretary who marked the cards would not give us a card and a tin each. He said that we did not come regularly.

'No, but we come when we can,' said Kenneth, 'and I'm sure we can get you some money.' So the man handed me the collector's card and, with a jocular remark that the gentleman always carried the luggage, gave the tin to Kenneth.

'Did *you* think what *I* thought?' he asked, when we got outside.

'Of course. It makes a whale of a reason for nosey-parkering round the village and asking questions,' I said. 'We shall have to be careful, because people do hate giving money except for hospitals and—'

'And the life boat,' he suggested.

'Yes. But I don't think people will be very interested in foreign missions. Our teacher in London told us that she gave up worrying about foreign missions when she found that they sent out the missionaries and the trade gin in the same ship.'

'What's trade gin?'

'I don't know, but that's what she said, so we'd better be careful not to argue and only start asking those people who won't turn nasty.'

'There are some we'll *have* to talk to, whether they turn nasty or not. We shouldn't argue with grown-ups, anyway. You only get your ears boxed if you do.'

Instead of going straight back to Aunt Kirstie for our Sunday dinner, we decided to call first on Aunt Lally.

'She goes to the Mission Hall regularly on Sunday evenings, or else to the Baptist Church in the town,' said Kenneth, 'so I think she is certain to give us something and it helps a lot if you can show people your card with somebody's name already on it and there's something to rattle in the tin. I know that from Cubs. A Boy Scout gave me the tip. "Shove a dud coin and a couple of buttons in before you start," he said, "and get one of your mates to sign the book." He said it always works, and it seems to, because I tried it, although I did put in a ha'penny of my own with the buttons and signed the card myself—well, it was a little notebook, actually—so as not really to cheat.'

So began our private Crusade in quest of Mr Ward's murderer. We only hoped we would not be called back to London before we had found him.

CHAPTER 14

The Hill Village Irregulars

Aunt Lally subbed up handsomely with three lovely great pennies. She wanted to save her threepenny bit (silver in those days) for Church collection, she said. Anyway, the pennies suited us because they set up such a suggestive response when we rattled them in the tin. Aunt Lally improved the occasion by telling us that we would get our reward in heaven hereafter by working for the Lord, and warned us on no account to go into the village public house with our collecting box.

'That belongs to the Salvation Army,' she somewhat ambiguously explained. When we went next door for our Sunday dinner with Aunt Kirstie the police were there again. Uncle Arthur was in the kitchen. He sent us straight up to the parlour and there the inspector took us all through our story again about how we had persuaded Poachy to dig up Mr Ward's body. The police sergeant sat at the table and checked off our replies against, I suppose, the previous statements we had made.

There was nothing new we could tell them. We repeated our stories of Mr Ward's digging operations in various places and our theory that the hermit might have hidden money or other treasure under the floor of the cottage; we told of Mr Ward's mad behaviour in the sheepwash and of the grave he had dug. They questioned us closely about this. What had made us think of a grave? Had we ever seen an open grave? What made us ask Poachy to help us? Why had we forced apart the bars in the iron fence which bounded the back garden? Who else ever went into the cottage?

We answered truthfully, although the questioning made me nervous. The inspector realised this because, as he got up to go, he said,

'It's all right, youngsters. We don't suspect you of doing anything wrong and we shan't be troubling you again.' To Aunt Kirstie he said, 'We'll see ourselves out, Mrs Landgrave. If anything else concerning Mr Ward should occur to you which you think may help us, I shall be glad to know.'

When he and the sergeant had gone, Kenneth said,

'We ought to have asked them if they'd like to give us something for our missionary box.'

'They'd have thought it cheek,' I said, 'and it doesn't do to cheek the police. You get sent to Borstal.'

After dinner we decided that Sunday afternoon was a bad time to go round the village asking for charity, because money given away on Sunday was for church collection, and anyway, all the grown-ups would be taking their Sunday afternoon siesta and would not be pleased at having to get up and answer the door, so, to repay Aunt Lally for her kind contribution to our missionary box, we went to her while she was doing the washing-up and asked for something Sundayish to read. That sent her happily up to her afternoon rest. We read for a bit, then we sneaked out into the garden to plan the morrow's campaign and draw up a list of people we wanted to question, but by the time Aunt Lally came downstairs again to wake grandfather and give him his tea we were back indoors with our Sunday pamphlets. She was very pleased with us.

When Monday morning came I think that, but for Kenneth, I would have abandoned our project. What had seemed such an amazingly good idea in Sunday school looked far less attractive at breakfast time on the following day. I said to my brother,

'Do you really think we'll do any good?'

'Of course we shall. Think, if we can beat the police at their own game!'

'But even if we do find out something important we shall have to tell it to them.'

'Not to them; not directly, anyway.'

'What shall we do with it, then? It won't be any good just keeping it to ourselves.'

'Of course not. We tell Mrs Bradley up at the manor. *She'll* know whether it's important enough to pass on. In fact, I vote we tell her everything we find out, whether it's important or not. I'll tell you something else, too. We might get hold of something to do with that other murder. You know, the girl who was at Lionel's sister's party.'

'Do you really think so?' I asked doubtfully.

'Well, we've put Mrs Grant on our list and we know Doctor Tassall visits her—she's his patient because of her ague she's always complaining about—and Doctor Tassall writes letters —I expect they're love-letters or some rot like that, you know...'

'Yes, to Amabel Kempson-Conyers. Do you wish *we* had a double-barrelled name?'

'Anybody can have one if they are stuck-up enough, I believe. We could call ourselves Innes-Clifton if we liked.'

I tried it over a time or two and then rejected it.

'I'd feel silly,' I said. 'But about Mrs Grant? She can't know anything worth much about Mrs Kempson and those people up at the big house.'

'We shan't know that unless we ask her. Then there's Old Mother Honour. Her shop is almost opposite the hermit's cottage. She must know something about who goes into it.'

'Well, so do we. Our Sarah and her lot, then us, then Mr Ward and now Poachy.'

'*And* the man who put Mr Ward in that hole and buried him. Suppose she knows who *that* was, eh? And suppose she told us, and we told Mrs Bradley, and she told the police! We might even get our names in the papers!'

'I wouldn't want that, unless they'd caught the murderer first and locked him up.'

'Well, they'd have done that, of course, on our information.'

So I committed myself to the enterprise and we began with

Mrs Grant. We found her sitting on her doorstep as usual rocking herself to and fro and moaning about her ague.

'I hab de ague bery bad, bery bad,' she told us.

'I'm sorry to hear it,' said Kenneth in a grown-up way, keeping the collecting-box behind his back, for we did not want to frighten her off before we had got any information out of her which she might possess. Besides, it was rumoured in the village that she was a Catholic, although, so far as was known, she never went to church. Anyway, I doubted whether she would give anything towards the Sunday school's Foreign Missions because, after all, she herself was a foreigner and might think it a cheek of the English to send out missionaries. She might even have feasted off a missionary in her earlier life, I thought. 'Still,' my brother went on, 'I suppose even the ague is better than being murdered.'

'Murdered? Mudder ob God, who is murdered?'

'Surely you know,' I said, taken aback, all the same, by what I believed to be a blasphemous exclamation. 'You heard about the girl at the sheepwash, and now Mr Ward.'

'Nobody don' tell me notting. No friends I got in dis place.'

'No, they're not a very friendly lot,' said Kenneth. 'We can tell you about the murders if you like.'

'You come in. I gib you glass ob good wine.'

'No, thank you all the same. We're Band of Hope,' I said, afraid that Kenneth was going to accept the invitation. 'Have you seen the doctor lately?'

'Doctor no damn good. I tell him not to come no more. I got no more letters to gib him.'

'Letters?' We pricked up our ears.

'Long time young lady send embelopes to me. Inside is letter in smaller embelope address to Doctor Tassall. It is an arrangement. He treat me free for my ague, I gib him his letters. Dey come first from France, den London, but no more. Young lady she don' write no more letters and I don' have money to pay doctor, so I tell him not to come no more, and he don' do notting for de ague, anyway. Now I go indoors, sit by fire. Goodbye.'

'Well, *that* wasn't much good,' said Kenneth, as we walked

on down the village street. 'Not that I expected much from her.'

'I think we ought to make a note about the letters,' I said. 'Letters are always important. Look at the letter Laurie wrote to Meg, pretending it came from his tutor. There was an awful row about that. And look at the letter that man in the pub wrote to Jellicoe that could have got Mike Jackson expelled when he biked over at night to pay the five pounds.'

'Tell Mrs Bradley about the letters, do you mean?' Kenneth was obviously impressed by my arguments, for, although he had not read *Little Women*, he, like me, had wallowed in the *Captain* magazine which was in bound volumes in our local public library at home, and especially did we love the school stories by P. G. Wodehouse.

'Well, I bet it's something nobody but Mrs Grant knows about,' I said. 'What only one person knows must be a secret of some sort and secrets, like letters, are always important.'

We walked on and then stopped outside the Widow Winter's house. She was on our list, but neither of us wanted to knock on her door.

'We could leave her till last,' said Kenneth, 'and then perhaps we shan't need her at all.' We went on to Mother Honour's, but all she said when she saw our box was,

'I'm here to take money, not give it. Out you get!'

So out we went. We stood outside the little post-office and looked at the tumble-down cottage across the road.

'She *must* know something,' said Kenneth. 'After all, her shop door is bang opposite. If only I hadn't put my ha'penny in this silly tin I could have bought some sweets and then perhaps she'd talk to us.'

'Not for only a halfpenny,' I said. 'We'd better try Miss Summers next, I suppose. She lives nearly opposite Mrs Grant, so we might hear something more about the letters.'

'They can't be all that important.'

'They must be, or else they wouldn't need to be kept so secret.'

'They wouldn't be about the murders, anyway. They might be love-letters. Something silly, anyway, I'll bet. I thought

Amabel was an awfully silly girl, didn't you? Besides, you and I used to have a secret post, don't you remember?'

'Yes, but it was only a shoe-box with a slit in the lid. Well, do we try Miss Summers or don't we?'

So we tried Miss Summers, but it was not any good. As soon as she spotted the collecting-box she said,

'You're the third lot that's come bothering me. Don't you know it's against the law to beg?'

'It isn't for ourselves,' said Kenneth.

'Don't you tell me that! You children are all the same. *You* know what to do with a hatpin, I'll be bound!'

'Well,' said Kenneth, when we got outside, 'if we didn't then, we do now, and it is in a good cause. Even Aunt Lally would agree to that.'

'You're not going to winkle out her three pennies, are you?' I asked, torn between excitement and terror. 'Wouldn't it be stealing?' (Stealing, to our minds, was a much greater sin than murder. The truth is, I suppose, that stealing came within our comprehension; murder, although we had had evidence of it, still did not.)

'Well, David took the shewbread when there wasn't anything else for his men to eat.'

'He didn't steal it, though. The priest gave it to him.'

'Well, Aunt Lally gave the pennies to us. She didn't say anything about missionaries when she put the money into the tin. We'll have to make it up later on, of course. If it wasn't in a really good cause I wouldn't do it. Let's get back to Aunt Kirstie's and get hold of a hatpin.'

All our fiddling and fidgeting, however, failed to produce a single coin. I was immensely relieved and I believe Kenneth was, too.

'Oh, well,' he said at last, when we returned the hatpin surreptitiously to the crown of Aunt Kirstie's best hat, 'I suppose it's really God's money and He's holding on to it. We'd better have one more go at people and it's no use funking it. We've got to try the Widow Winter.'

Greatly to our surprise we found the Widow Winter on the defensive when she answered our knock on her front door.

'Ef your grandad sent you,' she said, 'you tell hem et ent no good. Oi ent got et and that's a fact. Oi do know as how Oi'm a lettle bet be'oind-'and, but he'll get et when Oi gets moi next Lord George.'

We had no idea what she was talking about, but Kenneth dropped the collecting-box behind a bush in her tiny front garden and I said,

'Grandfather didn't send us. Could we just speak to you for a minute about the murders?'

'About the murders? Not about the rent?'

Light dawned on me. She was behind with her rent. I knew how people dreaded that. Eviction for non-payment of rent was all too common in those days, I suppose. We knew that the first thing our own mother did when father brought home his wages at the end of the week was to count out the rent-money and put it in the tea-caddy ready for the rent-man when he came on Monday morning. We realised, therefore, with the precocious intelligence of the children of the poor, that if the Widow Winter owed our grandfather even two weeks' rent we had the whip-hand of her, especially as being behind with her rent was the last thing she would want her neighbours to know about.

'Not about the rent. I expect grandfather will wait a bit longer,' I said. 'But we want to talk to you, please, Mrs Winter. We won't keep you long, but it's very, very important.'

'And about the murders?' Her long thin nose appeared to quiver with eagerness. 'Well, you better come enside, then.'

So, for the first and last time in our lives we penetrated into the forest of pot-plants from behind which she kept watch over the comings and goings of the village. The room was airless, stuffy and heavy with a smell of wet and decaying foliage. She asked us to sit down, but she herself remained standing at the window behind her barrage of plants, barely turning her head when she spoke to us. It seemed as though she could not bear to take her eyes off the village street, and the houses opposite her own, even for a moment.

'It's about Mr Ward,' I said. 'Aunt Kirstie's lodger, you know.'

'I ded hear as they dug hem up en the old cottage down the road. Murdered for hes money, Oi reckon.'

'For his money?' This, to us, was entirely a novel idea. 'But he didn't have any money.'

'Oh, dedn't he, though!' She sniffed importantly. 'Only went to the public every day of hes loife and took hes denner there as well as hes beer. Every four weeks he was en Old Mother Honour's lettle post-office a-changen of hes bets of paper Messus Kempson sent hem.'

'How do you know?' asked Kenneth.

'Talked to Messus Honour when Oi got moi Lord George dedn't Oi? Ferret and foind out, that be moi motto. Ef ee don't arsk ee don't learn, do ee? Don't you arsk questions when you be at school?—whech Oi do notece as you beant there thes mornen. Whoi not, then?'

This question ought to have non-plussed us, but we had agreed upon our answer to it if it was put to us, as we thought it might well be.

'Because the police and Mrs Kempson and an important lady called Mrs Bradley have asked us to help them and, in any case, our school is in London, not here,' I said glibly, for we had memorised and rehearsed this wording. The Widow Winter withdrew her gaze from the window long enough to give us a hard look, but all she said was,

'Oh, Oi see. Oi follered hem ento the shop one day to boi moiself a stamp and Oi seen hem get twenty pound acrorst the counter—just loike that! The post-offece in the town ded used to send Old Mother Honour the money special every month, Oi reckon, so as her could pay et out to hem. Her wouldn't never have all that money en the tell, and her'd have to gev et to hem when he handed over hes money-orders —four on 'em!'

This was a revelation to us. Twenty pounds! The largest amount we had ever seen at one and the same time was the five pounds our father received every Quarter Day for travelling expenses. As he always used his bicycle for getting about, the five pounds came in very handy indeed and we always felt immensely proud of him when he put them out on the kitchen table in front of mother and they laughed together with pleasure over them.

'Oi'll tell ee sommat else,' said Mrs Winter. Like so many lonely people (and, ostracised as she was in the village because of all the spying she did, I imagine that she was very lonely indeed) she talked to us as though we were her own age. 'You knows about the noight the young lady was kelled? Well, Oi 'adn't got off to sleep—Oi sleeps en the front room, see?—when Oi hears one o' them moty-cars go boy.

'"Oi knows the sound of that there," Oi says to moiself. "That be Doctor Matters' car," Oi says. "But 'twouldn't be hem, not at past ten o'clock," Oi says. "That'll be Doctor Tassall—ah, and what do he get up to weth old Mother Grant? Loike foine to know that, Oi'ud."'

'I expect he goes to look after her ague,' said Kenneth.

'Not wethout she paid hem, and *that* she can't afford, so what goes on? But now you lesten here. Oi be loyen awake, wonderen, and turnen Doctor Tassall over en moi moind, loike, when Oi hears *another* car, blest ef Oi don't. And who do ee thenk *that* was, then? Whoi, et was Mester Noigel Kempson, that's who et was. Knows hes car too, Oi does. "So what goes on?" Oi says to moiself. Woild young men, the two of 'em, Oi thenks. So Oi puts on moi wrapper and Oi sneaks down the stairs and Oi goes out to moi front gate and what do Oi see? Et's a lovely clear noight, not near what ee'd call dark, and Oi sees a beg shadder standen opposyte Messus Honour's.'

We hardly dared to breathe. This was true drama and greatly superior to anything Our Sarah had told the Sunday school children on the day after the murder.

'*Please* go on!' said Kenneth. 'What happened next?' Mrs Winter, sparing a second from her window-gazing to turn and shake her head, replied regretfully,

'Don't Oi wesh Oi knowed! Oi reckon et were a car, but whether et were Doctor Matters' car, or whether et were young Mester Noigel's car weth him or somebody else or hem *and* somebody else en et, es more nor Oi can tell ee.'

'You don't mean the girl they found down by the sheep-wash?' asked Kenneth.

'No better than she should a-ben, ef you arsk me! A proper lettle flebberty-gebbet. Must ha' ben. Out to meet some man or other, Oi reckon, and he done for her. But you wouldn't understand, at your age, and quoite roight as ee shouldn't. There've allus ben goens on and more goens on, and the gentry be worst o' the lot. Ah, and that young Doctor Tassall, too. Hem and hes Messus Grant!'

'We don't think Mr Ward was murdered for his money,' said Kenneth, 'but perhaps he found the treasure in the hermit's cottage and was murdered for that.'

'Treasure? What treasure?' Her long nose quivered again.

'Well, *something* must have been buried there, or why did Mr Ward dig up the floor?'

'Hem? Proper dotty-loike, weren't he? Touched en the head, Oi reckon.' She had scarcely at all ceased to keep vigil at the window and now she exclaimed: 'There's somebody new a-walken down the road! Now who would that be, Oi wonder? Look loike her as Oi seen en the Kempson's car a-comen back from the town station weth luggage an' all.'

'Do you mean Mrs Bradley?' asked Kenneth, jumping up from his chair.

'You keep out o' soight! You keep out o' soight!' cried Mrs Winter in agony. 'Nobody don't never see nobody watchen out moi front winder!'

'She's got a hope!' said Kenneth, when we were outside the front door and he had scooped up the money-box. 'Oh, well, if she owes her rent, it wouldn't be any good asking her for money.' We shot out of Mrs Winter's front gate and joined Mrs Bradley in the road. I thought she seemed pleased to see us.

'Well, well, well! The Baker Street Irregulars!' she said. At that time we had not read the Sherlock Holmes stories and so this quip was lost on us. Later I wondered how she knew or guessed that we had been doing—or trying to do—some detective work.

'How have you got on?' was her next question. 'And to

what extent, if any, has a good cause benefited from your questionable endeavours?'

We knew she was pulling our legs, but Kenneth answered truthfully.

'We've only got threepence ha'penny, and the ha'penny is mine. At least, it was mine before I put it in the box, and Mrs Honour won't answer any questions because we haven't any money to spend.'

'That is a deficiency which can be dealt with.'

'Oh, no!' I said, as she took a fat purse out of her skirt pocket. 'We're not allowed to take money.'

'This is not money; merely working expenses,' she said. I thought of father and his quarterly five pounds, and this did seem to put a different complexion on the matter. 'In a business concern,' she went on, 'it is quite usual for the partners to put up the capital and for others to take a salary and work for the firm until such time as they, too, are in a position to invest in it.'

We told her what had happened so far.

'Valuable information from Mrs Grant,' she commented, 'and a useful pointer from Mrs Winter. It was one which had already occurred to me, so I am glad to have an opinion which coincides with mine, especially as it comes from such a source. I imagine, from what I have heard about her from various persons, that what Mrs Winter does not know about what goes on in the village is, as the saying goes, not worth knowing. You have done well. As you probably thought, Miss Summers may have picked up gossip from the baker with whom, I am told, she has a platonic understanding. As for Mrs Honour, as you think and say, living, as she does, almost opposite the cottage in which Mr Ward was found, she must have something to report. Let me accompany you into these Hansel and Gretel dwellings and we will put the owners to the question.'

'That's what they used to call it when the Spanish Inquisition was working,' I said. 'We won't really torture Miss Summers, will we?'

'Nor Mrs Honour, I trust. Did you know that our English version of Hansel and Gretel is completely bowdlerised? In the original version collected by the brothers Grimm, no witch appears except the wicked step-mother, who is referred to not as a witch but as a fairy, albeit, we must suppose, a wicked one, and there is no house made of confectionery in the story. Hansel, in fact, is turned into a fawn after drinking from the third of the forbidden brooks and is cherished by his sister Gretel until the king who marries her catches the wicked fairy and makes her change Hansel back again. Well, never mind Miss Summers. Let us concentrate upon Mrs Honour.'

CHAPTER 15

Mrs Lestrange Bradley Again

It was clear that Margaret and Kenneth knew Mrs Honour's shop-window display off by heart and I feel sure that they could have played Kim's Game with the items with great success. This being so, we went inside the shop, as there was a further display within, so that comparisons could be made and merits weighed up and discussed.

While they were choosing what I was to buy for them, I entered into conversation with the shopkeeper and post-mistress concerning the stamps I should require to send a letter to America. Having settled this matter, I then purchased envelopes and notepaper and asked whether she did not think that the American police were more efficient than our own.

As I had hoped and anticipated, this proved to be an effective ploy, for she replied that, if they were not, she hardly supposed they would catch any criminals at all. I agreed with her and suggested that it was disgraceful that a woman like herself, living alone—that was a shot in the dark, but it found its mark—should be without police protection. She agreed and immediately confessed that she now felt extremely nervous at nights, since she knew that there was a fiend in human shape roaming about the village. She added that no one was safe.

'Must be a madman,' she said. 'Who with any sense in their head would kill first an innocent young lady who was not even known in the place, and then a nice, quiet gentleman like Mr Ward?'

'Oh, was he nice and quiet?' I asked. She assured me that he was and that he called regularly at her shop to buy snuff, for she had a licence to sell tobacco. He also used the post-office counter, she added, but only once a month.

'I suppose you cannot see from behind your counter which children or other people might ever have gone into the cottage where Mr Ward's body was found,' I remarked. She said that the police had asked her that, but she could tell them nothing except that some rude children occasionally came and shouted in at her doorway so that she was obliged to chase them away.

'The last lot ran into the cottage to get away from me, but that was weeks ago,' she said. 'I've seen nothing since.'

So the young Cliftons made their modest purchases, thanked me quite unnecessarily and we made out way up the slope to the house where they were staying. Having franked myself, so to speak, by purchasing their confectionery for them, I said that I should be interested to meet their aunt.

She proved to be a buxom, kindly woman, very different from the elderly and (I suspect) shrewish Mrs Honour, and when the children introduced me as a friend of Mrs Kempson —they had insisted upon taking me up the steps to the front door, although I am sure their usual entrance was by the side-way and the kitchen—Mrs Landgrave took me into the parlour and insisted upon giving me refreshment. We then got rid of the children and settled down to conversation about Mr Ward.

Yes, she said, he had been quiet enough and gave no trouble. She knew he spent time at the village public house, but declared that she had never seen him what she called 'the worse'. On the other hand, during the week or two before his death she had become increasingly worried about his idiosyncrasies. He had dug up their garden and her father's chicken-run and one day she had seen him come into the kitchen just as she had put the children's mid-day dinner on the table and had noticed that he was soaking wet up to his waistcoat and had great splashes of mud on his face.

Subsequently, although they had tried to hide the fact, she found that Kenneth's shorts and Margaret's cotton frock were also wet and muddy. When she discovered this and challenged them about it, they reported that they had seen Mr Ward standing in the sheepwash wielding a pickaxe. They had been alarmed and had hidden partly in the brook when he abandoned his strange occupation and appeared to be coming their way.

I had heard something of Mr Ward's pickaxe and spade-work from Mrs Kempson, who had had it from Mrs Landgrave, but I was glad to get it at first hand from the same (I thought) reliable source.

'Do you think,' I asked, 'that Mr Ward attacked somebody with either spade or pickaxe and was killed by that person in self-defence and subsequently buried in the hope that his death could be kept from the police?'

'I can't see him going for anybody,' she said, 'not unless he had gone out of his mind. He was always quiet and decent when he was here.'

'Yet you were sufficiently anxious about the state of his mind to contact Mrs Kempson,' I said. She explained that it was the children of whom she had been thinking.

'It isn't nice to have anybody that's a bit touched when you have children around,' she said. 'Besides, we thought Mrs Kempson ought to know.'

'Did you think it strange,' I asked, 'that Mrs Kempson did not accommodate him at the manor house? Surely she had plenty of room up there?'

But Mrs Landgrave refused, very properly, of course, to commit herself on either of these points, protesting that she had never thought about it and that she had been glad of the money which Mrs Kempson paid. This seemed to lead us to a dead end and I was about to thank her for the refreshment she had provided—a glass of very good cowslip wine and a biscuit—when a thought recurred to me. I say 'recurred', my dear Sir Walter, because in an earlier idle moment it had occurred to me one day when Mrs Kempson was describing her first meeting (after his lengthy absence) with Mr Ward. This thought was that it was difficult to reconcile the cool, hard-headed, somewhat cynical ex-convict which she had described to me, with the mentally deranged individual of quiet, inoffensive habits but eccentric behaviour pictured to me by Mrs Landgrave.

'Are you a suggestible person?' I asked her. 'I mean by that,' I explained, for I could see that she did not understand me, 'the kind of person who is apt to be influenced by the last speaker, for example.'

I was sure she would deny this, and she did. (People always do.)

'You're thinking of my sister Lally, the children's other auntie,' she informed me. 'I don't think anybody could make me change my mind once I'd made it up, except that sometimes, when I'm cross with the children, they can get round me, especially Ken, who is the most lovable little boy.'

'They are charming children,' I said. 'Well, then, Mrs Landgrave, if you are not suggestible, I would like to put a plain question to you and will wait while you consider your answer.'

'Oh, dear! You sound like that policeman,' she said. 'All right, then, you ask and either I'll answer truthfully or not at all.'

'Fair enough,' I agreed. 'Now Mr Ward was with you for just over five years, I believe. Did you ever wonder whether the man whom Mrs Kempson sent to you was the Mr Ward who carried out all that extraordinary delving?'

She stared at me, then she closed her eyes. She certainly took her time before she opened them again. Then she shook her head firmly.

'No,' she said decisively. 'He may have gone a bit wrong in his head, poor man, but it was the same gentleman. Turned up one afternoon with his little portmanteau of clothes and said he was Mr Ward and he believed it was all arranged he should stay with me.'

'Did Mrs Kempson accompany him to introduce him to you?' I asked, although I felt I knew the answer from the way she had described his arrival. She shook her head again.

'She didn't bring him nor did she ever come here to visit him,' she averred. 'All she did was to send me his money every week and him his money orders to cash at the post-office each month. I knew about that because the postman used to come before Mr Ward got up and I used to put the letter—it was the only one he ever got—by the side of his plate, and once he opened the envelope just as I brought in his eggs and bacon and one of the money orders fell out. I saw what it was, although he scuffled it up again all quick. I didn't see the amount and anyway that was no business of mine.'

I took my leave. She had given me something to think about. It seemed to me that another consultation with Mrs Kempson might be advantageous. Before I returned to Hill House, however, I thought I would pay a visit to the Widow Winter. From what the children had told me, it seemed that, if she chose, she could prove to be a valuable source of information about what I was beginning to think must be the pseudo Mr Ward.

She was all servility and unctuousness, a female Uriah Heep if ever I met one, and she invited me in without enquiring either my name or my business. I found out at once that, to some extent, she knew both. (I attempt to reproduce her remarks.)

'Do please to set down, ma'am,' she said, when she had conducted me into a small, airless room which smelt, although less attractively, like one of the hothouses at Kew Gardens. 'You well be the lady as es stayen up the hell weth the lady of the manor, and very glad she es of your company, Oi'll be bound.'

'Yes, Mrs Kempson and I are good friends,' I said, 'but it is not of her that I have come to speak.'

'Oi see you goen up the road with them cheldren of Messus Landgrave's. Dear little souls they be, and knows how to behave themselves, as there's others as don't. Ben to see Messus Honour, Oi reckon, and bought the cheldren some sweeties, as Oi seen them weth sherbet dabs and a bag what could have ben toffee. Oi *knows* you never went to Mess Summers, because her leves opposyte and Oi would have seen you go en there, wouldn't Oi? So ef the keddies had sweets et was from Messus Honour's, not as she could tell ee much, Oi'll lay. But et pays to be koind to lettle cheldren, don't et, ma'am?

The good Lord's lambs they be, when all's said and done. Oi ded hear as et was them as got that poor Poachy Leng to deg up that poor Mester Ward. What an experience for innocent cheldren! Enough to sour their loives on 'em, Oi do declare!'

'I do not think they saw the actual body, you know. They appear to have fled to their grandfather as soon as they realised what Mr Ling was digging up,' I said. 'It seems that the little girl had found one of Mr Ward's elastic-sided boots in the garden of that hideous cottage and jumped to the right conclusion as soon as Mr Ling uncovered the first signs of clothing on the cadaver.'

'To thenk of that, now! And Poachy Leng, as es hes mother's cross en loife—not but what Oi suppose we've all got one of *them* to trouble us—goen about the vellage as pleased weth hesself as ef he'd found a crock of gold instead of a poor murdered man!'

'Crocks of gold are only found at the foot of the rainbow, I believe,' I said.

She looked at me with a kind of ghoulish craftiness and observed,

'Oi reckon Mester Ward found a crock of gold, all roight, though not en that there old cottage.'

'How do you mean?' I enquired.

'Getten money out of Messus Kempson loike that! Ben en Mother Honour's, Oi have, when Oi see her push hem twenty pounds across her counter, and Oi was en Mess Summers' shop another toime when Oi see Messus Landgrave change a pound for a couple of loaves and a quarter of tea. Oi says to moiself as that must be some of the money as Mester Ward brengs en. Oi see the manor servant come to Messus Landgrave's proud as a lord on one of the carriage horses. Come every Froiday he ded, regular as clockwork, and et was on a Froiday, after he ben, as Oi was en Mess Summers' that toime. Oi knows as Arthur Landgrave, when he's en work, whech ent always, hem be'en a plasterer, gets paid of a Saturday, not a Froiday, so when Oi sees her change a pound on a Froiday, well, you know what to thenk, don't ee?'

'How do you know a servant comes to Mrs Landgrave's house on Fridays?' I asked.

'Her front railings stands a long way further out nor moine. Oi can't see her front door, but Oi can see who comes to her front gate. Oi see you and them cheldren go en a whoile ago.'

'So I suppose you could see Mr Ward leave her house when he went into the village to obtain his money. How did you know it came from Mrs Kempson?'

'Told ee of the servant what used to roide down to Landgrave's. He's the Lettlemore's fourth boy and Oi was en Mess Summers' when hes mother come en and Oi made a remark and she stared me down and called me a nosey old busybody, ef ever you heard the loike, and said p'raps Oi'd loike to know who posted a letter every month to Mester Ward and whether they posted et up on the London road or where. So then Oi knowed as sommat funny was goen on.'

'I suppose Mr Ward was an object of curiosity in the village,' I said. 'I know what he was wearing when he was found. Did he always wear elastic-sided boots?'

She launched herself into a full description of Mr Ward's appearance and I memorised it carefully so that I could repeat it to Mrs Kempson, although I did not think it would be of much help for purposes of comparison, since it was five years or more since she had seen what I had begun to believe was the *real* Mr Ward.

When I returned to Hill House I had to admit to her that I was as far off as ever from being able to elucidate the mystery of Mr Ward's death and burial, and then I asked whether she had been called upon to identify the body. She said that the Landgraves were to do that and would be called at the inquest which would be held on the following day, but that she also proposed to attend it, as it was known that she had been responsible for Mr Ward's support while he had been lodging with the Landgraves.

'You mean that the police know it?' I asked.

'Yes. I knew they would question the Landgraves, so I thought it better to come out with it,' she said. 'I did not want them to think there was any hole and corner business about the matter, since, of course, there was nothing of the sort. It was simply that I would not have Ward in this house.'

'What did Mr Ward look like when you met him?' I asked. 'Can you add anything to what you told me before?'

'Look like? I hardly remember. I suppose he was of average height, not noticeably tall or particularly short. He appeared to be of late middle-age, but I did not receive the impression that he was elderly. Apart from that, my memory fails me. He did not recall my brother to my mind and at first I doubted his claim. In fact, I still do, but it seemed so difficult and probably so expensive to prove him to be an impostor that I took the advice of my lawyers and did not attempt it. Besides, I will admit that something—his voice, I think—did stir some chord in my memory.'

'I think, you know, that it would be as well if you viewed the body. I could easily arrange with the authorities for you to do so,' I told her.

'Quite unnecessary,' she said, very firmly indeed. 'I have not set eyes on Ward since the day he made his impudent claim and should hardly recognise him again. Besides, if he has been residing with the Landgraves all this time, it *must* be the same man. I do not understand your questioning it.'

'Oh, I am not questioning it,' I said. 'You told me, when first we corresponded on the subject, that you had doubts of the man's true identity and that you had expressed those doubts to your lawyers. I suppose they are a reliable firm?'

'Reliable? Whatever do you mean? They are Price, Price, Whitstable and Price of County Street. They have been our family lawyers for years.'

'Ah, yes,' I said, having gained my objective, which was to find out the name of the firm without having to put a direct question to her. 'I have heard of them. No doubt they gave you the right advice.'

'It was the only advice they *could* give, considering the circumstances. It has saved me some thousands of pounds in costs, most likely. I was thankful to settle with Ward for his keep and his five pounds a week.'

'Surely a very modest claim for him to have made?'

'Oh, he wanted ten, but I beat him down.'

'But I thought you told me that this estate is entailed in the male line and that he was the rightful heir.'

'He did not wish to inherit. He could not have kept up the place or paid the servants. I received the impression that he was destitute or very nearly so.'

All this, of course, my dear Sir Walter, I had been told before, as you know, but it was helpful to hear it stated categorically all over again and it reinforced my resolution to contact Price, Price, Whitstable and Price and attempt to persuade one of the partners who had seen Mr Ward, when he visited them five years before, to come down and view the body so as to clear up any doubt as to whether their and Mrs Kempson's Mr Ward was also Mrs Landgrave's Mr Ward. It was the Widow Winter's attitude as well as the discrepancies in the attitudes and behaviour of the two, as described by Mrs Kempson and Mrs Landgrave which, interested me. It was quite likely that Mr Ward's mental state had deteriorated over five years, but the self-confident individual who had challenged Mrs Kempson and a reputable firm of London lawyers to prove he was not her brother scarcely approximated to what I had been told in the village of the silent, snuff-taking, idiosyncratic stranger who had lived with the Landgraves during the five years which preceded his death.

The next thing which happened, dear Sir Walter, was very curious indeed. In spite of my suggestion—made more than once—that I was trespassing overlong on her hospitality and that there was nothing I could do for her except to advise her to stay with her daughter and son-in-law in London for a bit if she felt lonely and nervous at the manor house, Mrs Kempson had repeatedly told me that she was glad of and grateful for my company. On the morning following my visit to Mrs Landgrave and the others in the village, however, she appeared to be excited by a letter which she had opened at the breakfast table.

'Oh, how very nice!' she exclaimed. 'It is from Nigel. He is able to spend a day or two with me and is coming tomorrow. Oh!' Her expression changed. 'He wonders whether he can have me all to himself, as he has much to discuss with me. Now that *is* a little tiresome of him. He knows I have you staying with me.'

I was glad enough of an excuse to take my departure from Hill House in order to obtain more freedom of movement than I could enjoy as Mrs Kempson's guest, so I agreed at once that it was only to be expected that when Mr Nigel had the opportunity to visit her, and as they saw so little of one another in the ordinary way, they should wish to be alone together. I suggested that I should take my leave of her immediately, so that the servants could tidy my room and have everything in apple-pie order for Mr Nigel's arrival on the morrow. She seemed greatly relieved and attempted explanations which I thought it better to cut short.

I am writing this letter, therefore, from Mrs Landgrave's pleasant, semi-detached villa residence, where I have arranged to take over (temporarily) Mr Ward's two rooms.

CHAPTER 16

The Wrongful Heir

Living in Mr Ward's quarters is a revealing and pleasant experience. The Clifton children have been summoned home and, although I miss their company, it is a relief to be alone and untrammelled. This is no place for infants who know as much as Margaret and Kenneth do, and I am also keeping an eye open on my own account, for matters are coming to a head.

You will hardly need to ask why I say this when I tell you of the latest developments in this murder-ridden village. As I mentioned in my last letter, the strange discrepancies between the account Mrs Kempson gave me of Mr Ward and the descriptions of him which I have had from the children and Mrs Landgrave suggested that I should bring in an outside witness to look at the body before the inquest on it was held.

I hoped to persuade Mrs Kempson to collaborate with me in getting her lawyers to appoint one of their number to come down. I even thought that curiosity might induce her to visit the town mortuary herself to assist in the identification, and this proved to be the case.

Fortunately my official standing with the Home Office meant that no obstacles were put in my way by the local people, and yesterday the three of us, Mrs Kempson, Mr Iowerth Price and myself were able to visit the town mortuary and inspect the features of the deceased.

They meant nothing to me, of course, so far as identifying

them was concerned, as I had never met the living Mr Ward, but the effect on my companions was instantaneous and, to me, gratifying. My hunch, if you care to call it that, although I prefer to have it thought that I had based it on sound psychological evidence, has proved to be correct. Neither the lawyer nor Mrs Kempson had any hesitation in declaring that the body they were shown was not that of the person who had introduced himself to them five years previously as Mrs Kempson's brother.

'No resemblance at all,' said Mrs Kempson firmly, and Mr Price agreed with her.

'And a man past middle age doesn't change all that much in appearance in five years,' he said. Yet, strangely enough, when Mrs Landgrave had been taken to view the body, without hesitation she had identified it, as her husband had already done—for they were taken separately to view it—as that of her late lodger.

'That is Mr Ward,' she said. Later, I asked Mrs Kempson, who was now both puzzled and shocked, which of the two men was more like what she remembered of her brother. I reminded her that she had said she did not recognise the first Mr Ward as such, and at their first meeting she had decided, until her lawyers advised against it, to contest his claim.

'So far as I remember my brother before he went to America,' she said, 'neither of them reminded me of Ward. I am beginning to think that neither of them *was* Ward, that the news of his death was correct and that these two men must have been friends or, more likely, fellow-prisoners of his. But how strange that they should both have conceived this idea of impersonating him, particularly as neither seems to have been prepared to claim the inheritance. Perhaps they dared not go so far as that.'

I suggested to her that she and Mr Price should give the police as full a description of the first Mr Ward as their memories would allow them to do. You will have come to the same conclusion as I did, I think, dear Sir Walter. Whoever had murdered Merle Patterson, there was no doubt in my own mind that the first Mr Ward had dramatically reappeared after five years and, for some reason known only to himself, had killed Mrs Landgrave's lodger, the second Mr Ward.

The verdict at the inquest was the anticipated one. Murder by person or persons unknown was a certainty, and so here we are, the police and I, with two unsolved crimes on our hands and a minor mystery to unravel as well.

As you will appreciate, it is difficult to envisage two murderers living in this small, obscure village, and yet there seems so little connexion between the two deaths as to suggest that they are entirely unrelated. The only link appears to be Mrs Kempson herself, but it is so weak that it hardly merits serious examination.

My first theory was that Mr Ward was murdered because he had been an involuntary witness of the slaughter of Merle Patterson, but what we learned at this second inquest has disposed of any such idea. The medical evidence now insists that Mr Ward was killed first, probably one or two days earlier than the young woman. This coincides, of course, with the Landgraves' assertion that Mr Ward had not slept in their house on either the Friday or the Saturday night.

Apart, therefore, from another theory of mine that Mr Ward himself (mentally unstable, as Mrs Landgrave had shown him to be) had murdered Miss Patterson wantonly and for no reason which would be entertained by a sane person, it is now clear that neither could he have been a witness to her death.

It seems reasonable to proceed, therefore, on the assumption either that there are two murderers living, if not actually in or near the village, at least with access to and knowledge of it, or that there is some connexion, most unlikely though it seems, between the two deaths. Otherwise there is a homicidal maniac in this neighbourhood, a most unwelcome idea.

Mrs Landgrave tells me that people are careful to lock their doors and fasten their windows at night, and to keep their children indoors in the evenings (although these are still long and light), and the gypsies are spoken of with more than the usual mistrust and suspicion.

There are two reasons why I am anxious to test my theory

that the first Mr Ward is a murderer. First, I cannot think why he has waited for more than five years before killing the second Mr Ward; second, and connected with it, I wonder why he permitted the second Mr Ward to live in comfortable lodgings (which I can assure you these most certainly are) with good food and five pounds a week to spend as he pleased, when he himself might have been enjoying these benefits. One is forced to the conclusion that he had to be seen and known in haunts other than the village street and public house, and that his plans required a substitute in Mrs Landgrave's reputable home.

I should be grateful to have the benefit of your thoughts upon all this, as the experience of a great advocate would be most valuable in such a puzzling case. The explanation of its mysteries may be staring me in the face and is probably perfectly simple, but at the moment it is baffling the police as well as myself and there is talk of calling in Scotland Yard. For more reasons than one, such a proceeding would be quite in order, especially as the dead girl was a Londoner and so the solution of one of our problems may well lie in London and not in this village.

It might be worth while to remember that on the night of Merle Patterson's murder five persons, not including little Lionel, have no alibi, so far as we know, for the time of that crime. Doctor Tassall was called out to a confinement, Nigel Kempson went into the town to pick up the photographer, Mrs Kempson went upstairs (she says) to bed and Mr and Mrs Conyers retired (they say) to their own quarters.

I am grateful to note, dear Sir Walter, that your mind marches with mine. Since my last letter there have been some interesting developments. Scotland Yard have been in touch with New York and there seems no doubt now that the woman who wrote to Mrs Kempson was right and that the real (or shall we call him, for the sake of clarity, the third) Mr Ward died out there as the woman stated.

I have decided, therefore, to drop the enquiry into Mr Ward's death (I mean, by this, the murdered Mr Ward) and to concentrate on the death of Merle Patterson. The problem here, as you point out, is to determine whether she was killed in her own right, so to speak, or whether she was mistaken, as we have suggested, for Lionel Kempson-Conyers.

I obtained the Pattersons' address from Mrs Kempson, who had issued the invitation to the birthday party to Merle's brother, and went to see them at their London home. It was obvious they have not recovered from the shock of their daughter's death but were anxious to do anything in their power to bring her murderer to book.

From them I obtained the address of the school where their son is a junior master and here, my dear Sir Walter, the story takes a most unhelpful turn. The young man is as anxious as his parents are to have his sister's killer apprehended. Unfortunately his evidence has blown what I thought was my case completely to pieces.

He states that it was quite untrue that he had received an injury on the cricket field which had left him temporarily incapacitated. He had accepted the invitation to the party and had fully intended to drive his three young female friends to Hill House when he received a letter from his sister. In it she begged him to think of some way in which she could get herself invited to the party. Not to weary you with unnecessary details, the fact was that she had been engaged to young Doctor Tassall before he met and fell in love with Amabel Kempson-Conyers.

The consequence was that Doctor Tassall had asked her to release him. Amabel must have known of the engagement, since she and Merle moved in the same circles in London where, you will remember, the Conyers have a flat, and young Patterson says that it was to save herself the embarrassment of a meeting and perhaps an acrimonious confrontation that Amabel had not invited his sister to the party.

What Merle wanted, it appears, was to talk face to face with Doctor Tassall, presumably either to plead with him or to point out the error of his ways. Well, it was a simple matter to get another young master to telephone that Patterson had been struck on the knee at cricket and to suggest that his sister should transport the three girls in his stead. His parents, of course, had no reason to disbelieve the story about his injured knee, so that his sister achieved her objective in the simplest possible way, by virtue of her brother's help.

She knew that Doctor Tassall was to attend the gathering, as Mrs Kempson had included a list of guests with each invitation, a fact of which Patterson had apprised his sister. What neither of them realised was that when Doctor Tassall received his own guest-list he probably took fright when he saw the name of his jilted fiancée's brother on it and, deeming discretion the better part of valour in a possibly embarrassing situation, had invented (I think) a fictitious maternity case which would give him the opportunity to leave the party at an early hour and not to return until he expected it to be over and the guests dispersed to their homes.

What he felt when not the brother but the ex-fiancée turned up, I do not suppose he would tell me, even if I asked him. His disappearance from the scene, however, does seem to explain why Merle Patterson haunted the grounds that night. Undoubtedly her intention was to waylay him on his return and discuss matters (whether amicably or otherwise) with him where they would neither be overlooked nor overheard.

This, I know, puts some suspicion on Doctor Tassall of having caused Merle's death, but this only holds good if Doctor Tassall knew that it was Merle out there in the grounds. If the murderer (whoever he was) mistook Merle in her disguise for Lionel Kempson-Conyers, then, to my mind, that murderer would not have been Tassall, but somebody who wanted to get *Lionel* out of the way. As this 'somebody' is most unlikely to have been the child's grandmother or either of his parents, as I believe I indicated in one of my earlier letters, that now leaves us either with Nigel Kempson or with somebody the cricketing lists call *A. N. Other*, who is most unlikely to be Doctor Tassall.

So these are the problems as I see them, and in an effort to solve them I have followed my visits to Merle's parents and her brother by attempting to discover whether Doctor Tassall had been called out on a genuine case that evening and whether Nigel Kempson had made any real attempt to pick up the photographer. Up to that point I had met neither of them and had been able to form no opinion of their characters or dispositions. Not that that, in itself, means much. It is said that every person has it in his power to write at least one book and that we all hold the life of at least one other person in our hands. Both are terrifying thoughts and I do not know which is the more alarming!

I decided to tackle the young men on what I felt was my home ground as well as theirs; that is, I planned to hold both interviews in Hill village, but to give myself a slight advantage in the case of Doctor Tassall by conducting his at my newly-acquired lodgings at Mrs Landgrave's and to yield a similar slight advantage to Nigel Kempson by seeing him at Hill House, where Mrs Kempson was expecting him for the week-end.

To my pleasure, (for, having no pretensions to good looks of my own, I appreciate them the more in others) both turned out to be personable young men, Kempson bright-haired and with the kind of blue eyes I have learned to mistrust, Tassall with dark hair and grey eyes and a look of recklessness which I would not normally associate with the possessor of a medical degree, whether or not he plays Rugby football. Nigel Kempson, I understand, is thirty years of age; Tassall is twenty-six and has been assistant to Doctor Matters here for nearly a year.

His association with Amabel Kempson-Conyers dates, he tells me, from a meeting he had with her in Paris early in her year at a finishing school, when he was instrumental in rescuing her from the amorous advances of two *apaches* in a quarter of the city into which she should not have strayed. What he himself was doing in such an unsavoury neighbourhood I did not ask.

Having heard from the Clifton children of the (obviously) clandestine correspondence which had gone on between himself and Amabel, mostly before she arrived at Hill House, I mentioned this to him.

'Oh, damn!' he said. 'Has that old Maltese woman been

talking? Anyway, it wasn't by my wish that she was made a go-between. It was Amabel's idea. Young girls are always romantic in that sort of silly way.'

My experience of modern young women did not incline me to agree with him, but I did not say so. I suggested that with one letter at least he had not acceded to Miss Kempson-Conyers' wishes.

'You gave it to the Clifton children to post,' I said. He laughed.

'Everybody seems to split on me,' he said, 'same as young Lionel splits on everybody, poor kid. Anyway, that particular letter was merely to tell Amabel that I intended to accept her grandmother's invitation to the birthday party, but not to count on me because, ten to one, I should be called out on a case.'

'Ah, yes, to avoid meeting your ex-fiancée's brother,' I thought, 'and you were even more thankful that you had planned an escape route when it was the young woman herself who turned up!'

I thought this, but did not say it, and my silence seemed to put him out of countenance. After a pause, during which we continued to sum each other up, he went on:

'Well, quite early in the evening I *was* called out. Mrs Collins was having her first and, although I guessed it was a false alarm, I excused myself to Mrs Kempson and hopped off. When I got back, there was all this fuss about Miss Patterson having gone missing.'

'Your ex-fiancée,' I said, deciding at this point to bring my knowledge of his affairs into the open.

'Oh, well, yes,' he said. 'Yes, that's right. It was only a boy and girl affair, you know. Once I had found Amabel it blew itself out.'

'Not, perhaps, from Miss Patterson's point of view.'

'Oh, well!'

'But it wasn't well, was it? Miss Patterson took it badly. You had managed to elude her in London, but when her brother received his invitation to Miss Kempson-Conyers' birthday party it included a list of guests with your name on it. Miss

Patterson then got her brother to yield up his place to her, knowing that, when she arrived as the *chauffeuse* of her brother's car, Mrs Kempson would feel bound to ask her to stay. I imagine that a very disgruntled young woman stood about in corners and watched you dancing with Amabel Kempson-Conyers until you thought it best to execute a strategic retreat.'

'No, no! Honestly! I *was* called out.'

'If that is your story,' I thought, 'we shall find out whether or not you are wise to stick to it.'

He looked at his watch and exclaimed that he was due in the surgery in five minutes' time. From the front window (for my sitting-room faces the village street) I watched him unhitch his horse and canter away. I am reluctant to think of him as a murderer. Besides, even supposing he had killed Merle Patterson, there seems no reason why he should also have murdered Mr Ward unless the latter had been an eye-witness of the first killing, and this, as the medical evidence has now established, is quite impossible, otherwise we might be that much further on in our enquiries.

Doctor Tassall had made one helpful remark during our conversation, although I doubted whether, in the end, it would prove to have very much significance. Even if his call to the pregnant Mrs Collins turned out to be as mythical as I was inclined to think it was, it did not necessarily mean that he had been determined to lie about it in order to give himself time and opportunity to commit murder. I still felt that the call was far more likely to have been for the reason I have already postulated; that is, in order to get out of an embarrassing situation at Hill House. I was prepared, therefore, to keep an entirely open mind on his behalf.

I did not know at the time whether Mrs Collins was a village woman or whether she lived in the town, but I did not think I should experience much difficulty in finding her. I did not want to ask Doctor Tassall for her address, this for obvious reasons, but to Doctor Matters I was unknown and the woman's name and address were certain to be among his files, even though theoretically she was now Doctor Tassall's patient.

A telephone call seemed the best way of making contact with Doctor Matters. I mentioned Mrs Kempson's name, which was politely but cautiously received.

CHAPTER 17

No Alibis

In the end Doctor Matters suggested that I should call and see him. He said that, owing to his advanced years, he rested for an hour and a half every afternoon while Doctor Tassall was out on the rounds and that he would expect me at a quarter to three.

He lived in a detached, creeper-covered residence about halfway between the village and the town and he received me in a ground-floor room whose furniture had seen better days, but which had a pleasant outlook on to a colourful, untidy, extremely long garden.

He took my hand and then waved me to a chair, took the one opposite, leaned forward and looked me over as though I were a patient he suspected of malingering in order to obtain a medical certificate to remain away from work.

'Well,' he said, 'you look healthy enough to me.'

'Quite,' I replied, 'but it is not about my health that I came to consult you.'

'I don't support charitable enterprises.'

'I am wary of them myself. Allow me to come to the point.'

'Dear me!' he said, his less than benevolent gaze becoming hostile. 'Are you one of these troublesome women who think they ought to have equal pay with men?'

'I have been adequately paid for some years. I am also, like yourself, a medical practitioner. Perhaps you would care to see my credentials,' I retorted.

'No need,' he said shortly. 'You wouldn't offer them if you didn't have them. What do you want?'

'I want to know whether your patient, Mrs Collins, has had a baby within the past three weeks.'

'Paternity order?'

'Not so far as I am aware. I want to know whether Doctor Tassall, your assistant, attended her confinement and on what date.'

'Why? Does he say he did? Did the careless young fool lose the baby? Is he suspected of any kind of unprofessional conduct? What the devil *is* all this?'

'It concerns a possible charge of murder.'

'You can't convict a medical man of murder, even if he kills mother and child.'

'If you would be kind enough to look up your files? I assure you that it is of the utmost importance. Doctor Tassall is not suspected of killing Mrs Collins, nor her baby. It must be established, however, for his sake, that he *did* visit Mrs Collins late in the evening of last Saturday fortnight when he was called out from a birthday party at Hill Manor House.'

'What did you mean about a charge of murder? Young Tassall is a butterfly and a jackanapes, a trifler with young women's affections, a parasite and an arbutus, but he wouldn't murder anyone except in the course of duty and *that*, as I've already asserted, can't be held against him.'

'The murder of a young woman with whose affections he had trifled could be held against him,' I pointed out, picking up my cue, 'so the sooner you provide him with an alibi the better.'

'God bless my soul!' he said. 'I suppose you're serious?'

'I am officially concerned with the case as the accredited representative of the Home Office, because I am its consultant psychiatrist.'

'Oh? One of those....'

'Quacks?'

'No, no, of course not. I—let me see. Did the maid bring me your card? Yes, yes, here it is. Dear me! Oh, dear, dear me! Yes, of course, of course. And you want to consult our files. What was that date again?' I gave it to him. He had no filing cabinet, so he pulled out various drawers in a large desk and groped and fumbled among the miscellaneous contents, muttering to himself as he threw some of them on to the floor, 'List! List! There's a list of patients somewhere, I know there is! Ah!' he exclaimed at last.

Apparently he had found what he was looking for. He produced out of the miscellany a set of handwritten papers pinned together at the top left-hand corner, handed it to me and said,

'Look for yourself. I don't remember the name of Collins, now I come to think of it. Don't believe there's a family called Collins on our books.'

To cut the story short, Sir Walter, there was not. I left Doctor Matters after thanking him and apologising for cutting into his rest-time and rang up the inspector from a public call-box in the town. I told him of my researches and suggested that a call on Doctor Tassall might yield some information.

'Yes,' said the inspector, 'we're keeping him in mind. Looks as though his alibi has gone bust. We would have followed it up ourselves, the way you have done, if we could have shown he had any motive for killing Mr Ward, or any reason to have known there was a ready-dug grave in that cottage. You see, we are proceeding on the assumption that whoever killed the girl killed Ward.'

This argument had considerable force, for we had agreed that the strong probability was that the same person or persons had committed both murders and that the connexion with Hill House was too obvious to be ignored.

I then returned to Doctor Matters' house.

'I think I should warn you,' I said, 'to expect a visit from the police.' This time the old gentleman was uneasy, not belligerent.

'That boy!' he exclaimed. 'A young rascal! A scallywag! A flibbertigibbet! Yes, and more. But he's well qualified, madam, good at his job. Takes a lot of work off my shoulders. Popular with the patients. No murderer, madam, I assure you.'

'Yours, judging from the list of patients you allowed me to examine, is not a large practice, I believe, Doctor.'

'A country practice only, madam, but quite large enough for me, and, in any case, I admit it is picking up since young Tassall joined me.'

'I am surprised that so restless and talented a young man, if one may so interpret your description of him, is not more inclined to work in the metropolis.'

'He had quarrelled with his godfather, who had subsidised him for some years while he was studying for his qualifications. Something about jilting a girl whom Lord Kirkdale thought a suitable match for him. Took up with the Kempson granddaughter and had his allowance withdrawn. Couldn't afford his own practice. Glad to earn a pittance from me without having to buy himself in. No expectations, you know. Irresponsible young fellow.'

'And glad to be near Amabel Kempson-Conyers at such times as she came to visit her grandmother,' I thought, 'but perhaps not irresponsible where his patients are concerned.'

Well, since my last letter, in which you learned that young Doctor Tassall appears to have no alibi for the time and date of the murders, I have continued my burrowings and have come up with another *gradu diverso, via una*. In other words, our other chief suspects also cannot produce acceptable alibis. Neither the police nor I have seriously suspected Mrs Kempson or Mrs Conyers unless either of them had a male accomplice, since we hardly think that the interment of Mr Ward, even though he appears to have dug his own grave, was the work of a woman, nor is the murderer's method of dispatching his victims a likely one for a female to have employed. This I think I have already mentioned. In any case, I am not concerning myself at the moment with the death of Mr Ward.

Mr Conyers, I suppose, must remain on our list, since his only alibi for the time of Miss Patterson's murder rests solely on his wife's assurance that he was with her the entire evening, first at the birthday revels and later in his own quarters. This,

I know, is against my previous judgment, but that depended largely upon Lionel Kempson-Conyers' being the proposed victim.

Well, Mr Conyers claimed, as we know, to have retired to his own part of the house. As he did not even ring for a drink, there is nothing to substantiate this claim and for the present we must ignore it, although my commonsense still tells me that it is almost certainly true.

With Mr Nigel Kempson, however, we are on different and much safer ground and, not to weary you with overmuch repetition, his alibi no longer holds water, but is as full of holes as a domestic colander. In brief, this is what happened.

It seemed to me, that in this interesting but baffling case, there might well be a nigger in the woodpile. I turned the thought over in my mind and fastened upon a very minor but maybe a significant mystery. I wondered why the photographer had not kept his appointment to visit Hill House on the night of Miss Kempson-Conyers' birthday party.

The arrangement had been that Mr Nigel Kempson was to pick him up in the town at an appointed meeting-place at about eleven p.m. and convey him by car to the manor house. Apparently he did not turn up at the rendezvous and Mr Nigel, having waited for a considerable time, returned without him.

It seemed strange to me that a professional photographer, having contracted to take a number of pictures in the house of so wealthy a woman as Mrs Kempson, had not kept what promised to be a very lucrative assignment, so I decided to make some enquiries.

My problem, and that of the police, was that there was no apparent reason why the same person should have committed both the murders. Added to this was the mystery of there having been (it seemed) two Mr Wards, both false, and the strange fact that nobody could have known beforehand (again it seemed) that Miss Patterson would attend the party in place of her brother except the two Pattersons and their parents.

Apart from this, the absence of the photographer made him

as much or as little of a suspect as anybody else, but, at any rate, he appeared to be a person whose movements should be more fully investigated.

As Mr Nigel had gone back to his London flat, I returned to Hill House and asked Mrs Kempson to repeat to me all that she could remember of the arrangements for the photographer's visit. She was only too anxious to find a scapegoat outside her own family, for she fully realised the implications suggested by the absence from the festivities of Mr and Mrs Conyers, herself and Mr Nigel at what must have been the time of Miss Patterson's death. She had previously done her best to impress upon me that Doctor Tassall was also out of her house at that time, and I knew that he had lied about his call to a maternity case. Perceiving my new drift, which might implicate the photographer, she proved more than willing to give me all the information she could.

She produced the photographer's typewritten reply. In it he regretted that a previous appointment would prevent him from attending at Hill House on the evening in question unless he could add a return taxi fare to his bill. To this Mrs Kempson had replied that, as the taxi would be kept waiting, presumably, while the photographs were being taken, and as it appeared that this would be a lengthy process, since her grand-daughter had arranged for a number of group photographs, as well as some individual portraits, to be taken, Mr Nigel Kempson would meet him outside the cinema in Broad Street, convey him to the house by car and take him back when the session was over.

This arrangement had been made over the telephone and the photographer had agreed to it, but there was nothing in writing.

I asked her whether the suggestion to pick up the photographer had come originally from Mr Nigel. She replied that it had not, and I wondered whether he had resented her high-handed assumption (as I saw it) that he would be willing to absent himself from the party for an hour or more merely to satisfy Miss Kempson-Conyers' whim and Mrs Kempson's wishes.

The photographer's address was at the top of his letter, so I went to see him.

I do not know why I had expected him to be a young man. He was nothing of the kind, but is, I should imagine, at least fifty years of age. When I announced that I had come from Mrs Kempson he looked hopeful and said, 'Oh, she's going to do something about it, then?'

'About what?' I asked.

'Why, me hanging about in Broad Street best part of an hour,' he replied, 'waiting to be picked up.'

'But you were not there at the right time.'

'Who wasn't?'

'You weren't. Mr Nigel Kempson waited for you, but you did not appear.'

'Who didn't?'

'You didn't.'

'You've got it the wrong way round, I'm afraid, madam. It was Mr Kempson didn't show up, not me,' he said. 'I would have written to Mrs Kempson to claim something for my time and the loss to me of not taking the photographs, but I reckoned she had enough on her plate with that poor girl getting murdered and Mrs Kempson's name in the papers and everything, so I thought I'd bide my time before I put it to her that she'd let me down.'

'I think we had better get this quite clear,' I said to him. Well, there was nothing to shake his story. He produced Mrs Kempson's letter and a copy of his own reply ... 'I keep copies, madam, mine being a chancy business and people sometimes in no hurry to settle up, so I like to have a record of the whole transaction' ... and he gave me the gist of the subsequent telephone conversation. He then said:

'Of course, that's the weak point, so far as I'm concerned, madam. I haven't anything in writing to say that Mr Nigel Kempson was to pick me up and nothing about the time or the place. I jotted them down, but that's not evidence, is it? And even if it was, I wouldn't have a case to take to court, I don't reckon, even if I was prepared to go as far as that, which, between ourselves, I would not be.'

'Just give me an account of what happened from the time you left your last appointment that evening and the time you decided that Mr Nigel Kempson was not going to put in an appearance,' I suggested.

The appointment, it appeared, had terminated at the Assembly Rooms in the Town Hall after he had taken photographs of the guests who attended a banquet there. He had taken three pictures in a matter of minutes. This was at half-past nine. From then until nearly ten o'clock, he and his assistant had been occupied in taking orders for copies of the photographs and had met with what he called 'about the usual run of luck' in selling the photographs later and in the matter of drinks.

They had then packed up their paraphernalia and he himself had crossed the road for another drink at the *Goat and Grapes* before that hostelry closed at ten-thirty, while his assistant had returned to the studio with the camera and so on. When the bar closed, the photographer, being known to the landlord as a personal friend, had been taken behind the bar to the back premises of the inn for a private drink which, incidentally, he would pay for on the morrow.

'It was to use up the half-hour before Mr Kempson was to pick me up,' he explained, 'but just in case he should be early, I went along to stand outside the cinema at ten to eleven, not to keep him waiting.'

'Ah, yes. You can prove this, of course,' I said. He did not put up any pretence of not understanding me.

'You surely don't think *I* killed that poor young creature and *that's* why Mr Kempson didn't pick me up at eleven, do you?' he said. 'He never turned up, I tell you, and that's why I turned it in at midnight and went home, and pretty cheesed off I felt, I don't mind telling you. Well, I didn't think I ought to 'phone up at that time of night and the next day was Sunday and then, when I 'phoned on Monday morning, a policeman answered and told me to ring up later, as Mrs Kempson could not talk to anybody. Then, of course, it was in the local paper all about the murder, so I wouldn't bother her, like I said.'

'Yes, I see,' I said. 'Can you think of anybody who might

have seen you standing outside the cinema waiting for Mr Nigel?'

'There were any number of people coming out of the cinema when it closed down at eleven. Some of them must have noticed me. Look here, are you to do with the police?'

'Sufficiently so for your purpose. I shall tell them about this interview and then they may contact you and make any enquiries they think fit.'

'You think I've been lying?' He could have sounded belligerent, but, as a matter of fact, he appeared to be alarmed. 'I assure you, madam, I've told you nothing but the truth. If Mr Kempson says he came to the cinema and didn't find me, *he's* the liar, not me. Hang it all, treat me fair! Which is more likely?'

'You have a point there, perhaps.'

'I never even knew the young girl.'

'Perhaps Mr Nigel is in a position to claim the same thing. However, it will be to your advantage to go to the police yourself and tell them what you have told me.'

'You don't mean I'm *really* suspected?' he said, looking even more alarmed.

'At the moment, neither less nor more than others,' I replied. His alarm had impressed me to some extent. I did not suspect him of murder. I *did* suspect that he had something to hide.

I went straight to the police station. The inspector was in his office dealing with various documents, but he received me courteously and asked what he could do.

'I want to know whether a telephone call came for Mrs Kempson while you were at Hill House on the Monday after Miss Patterson was murdered, Inspector.'

'Yes, there was a call.'

'Ah!'

'From the young lady's father.'

'Nobody else?'

'Nobody else. He was very distressed, of course, and asked what we wanted him to do. He said that his wife was in a state of collapse, but if he could be of any help he would come over. I advised him to stay put and we would let him know about the inquest, as his daughter would have to be identified formally.'

'And you are positive that there was no other call for Mrs Kempson that day?'

'What *is* all this, ma'am?'

'Probably nothing of importance,' I said. 'I wondered whether the photographer had rung up to explain why he had not come to the house to take the pictures at the birthday party.'

'No, he didn't ring, ma'am.'

I could not understand why the photographer had told me such a lie. I went to the Town Hall. It is a pretentious but ugly building which mars an otherwise charming street. The porter on duty enquired my business in a civil manner, so I asked him whether he had been on duty at the banquet of which I mentioned the date. It appeared that he had.

'I believe some photographs were taken,' I said.

'While he was sober, lucky enough,' said the porter. 'When he left I had to help him down the steps and then blowed if he didn't go tacking away across the street to the *Goat and Grapes*. Good thing there wasn't no traffic about. I watched him across and I thinks to myself as he'll be lucky if Bill Ballock serves him, the state he's in when he leaves here. When the photographs and the orders was all took, I reckon they give him a skinful in the mayor's parlour, 'cos, when I see him off, happy wasn't the word for it. He could still stand on his feet, just about, but I reckon that was instink, not intention.'

I crossed the road to the *Goat and Grapes*. At that hour it was empty except for a pot-boy polishing glasses. I asked to speak to the landlord and a Dickensian character of jovial aspect appeared. He remembered the night in question perfectly well, but for reasons quite unconnected with the murder.

'I always do pretty well when there's a "do" on in the Town Hall,' he informed me. 'Some of 'em come in before it starts, so as to get themselves into the mood, like, and if I'm still open when it's over, some of 'em comes in for a night-cap, as you might say.'

I mentioned the photographer.

'I understand he belonged to the night-cap contingent,' I said.

'Then you understand wrong,' said the landlord promptly. 'He comes in here in a state which I should describe as unfortunate and I refused to serve him.'

'He did not get anything to drink here?'

'He did not, madam. Do you think I want to lose my licence? I told him I was shutting up shop and he'd best go home and sleep it off.'

'You did not take him behind your bar and minister to him in your back room?'

The landlord stared at me incredulously.

'Who's been telling you *that* tale?'

'It was rumoured. You deny it, then?'

'If you wasn't a lady I'd do more than deny it; I'd add a few rude words to make my meaning clear.'

'So what happened to him?'

'My pot-man found him laid out sleeping it off in the gents when he went to hose out on the Sunday morning, but whether he'd been there all night, well, that I couldn't undertake to say.'

Intriguing, don't you think, dear Sir Walter?

CHAPTER 18

The Penny Drops

As you will realise, dear Sir Walter, the result of my investigations provided us with four lines of enquiry, for, after my meeting with the photographer, the police and I were pursuing our ends in even closer association than before.

The situation which confronted us was not, as so often happens in cases of murder, the necessity to break down alibis, but to establish them. Among our suspects, as I saw it, four had to be cleared and one retained.

'Psychology first,' said the inspector. 'I'm a great believer in it since one of your lot, ma'am, if I may so refer to a body of learned ladies and gentlemen in whom, usually, our lot don't place much confidence, was able to clear my little girl of a charge of thieving from another child at her school. Not that I'm all that sold on it in a general way, you understand, because, as it seems to me, psychology is more concerned with finding excuses for the criminal than getting him committed on a charge.'

Having obtained *carte blanche* from him, I considered my suspects all over again. Two of them, the photographer and Mr Conyers, I decided to ignore for the time being. Neither was at all likely to have had a motive for killing Merle Patterson and the only possible reason which Mr Conyers could have had for murdering Ward was that he thought him a threat to little Lionel's inheritance. As, according to Mrs Kempson, the estate was more or less of a white elephant, this motive seemed inadequate. Lionel would get the money anyway.

I turned my attention again to Doctor Tassall. It seemed time to put the cards on the table. I sent a note to the surgery to ask him to spare a few minutes on his next round or as soon as was convenient, to pay a call on Mrs Landgrave.

That this was a deceitful move intending to disarm him I freely admit. However, if he was a murderer, the nicer scruples were out of place; if he was an innocent man he had nothing to fear or, at this late stage in the proceedings, nothing to hide from me. The mere fact that he was suspected—if he did not know it already—should be sufficient, I thought, to make him willing to talk.

From my window on to the street I saw him arrive. I opened the front door to him myself and led him into my sitting-room.

'Are you the patient?' he enquired.

'There is no patient for you, but possibly one for me,' I replied. He did not pretend to misunderstand me.

'Any police hidden behind the arras?' he asked, with an attempt at flippancy which was bold but not convincing.

'No police, but I believe Mr Landgrave is within call.'

'Oh, yes. Bit of a bruiser, isn't he?'

'I believe he has the reputation of being a man of his hands.'

'I accept the hint. Well, if I'm the patient, what is your diagnosis?'

'I cannot make one until you have answered my questions.'

'Right. I haven't time for verbal sparring, so fire away, please. I've a number of calls to make.'

'It is about the one you *didn't* make that I should like to question you.'

'I don't have to incriminate myself, you know.'

'You could not do so at this particular interview, since there are no witnesses.'

'You don't think the police would accept your word against mine?'

'Not as proof positive. As a base for future enquiries I think they might. Now, Doctor Tassall, it ill becomes me, perhaps, to tell you that the best way you can help yourself is to tell the truth, but I believe that it would be in your own interests to do so. It was easy enough to find out that there is no such patient as Mrs Collins on your list.'

'Easy enough to find that out, yes. So what?'

'So I can think of various reasons why you left the birthday party so early that night.'

'Oh, yes? Are you going to tell me what they are?'

'Certainly, and leave you to indicate the right one.'

'And suppose I select the wrong one?'

'It will take me a little longer to find out which is the right one, that is all.'

'I see. Do you like answering riddles?'

'Propound one.'

'Try this, since you are trying to get me hanged. "There was a man made a thing, and he that made it did it bring, but he 'twas made for did not know whether 'twas a thing or no."'

I was familiar with the riddle, so I said:

'I believe you are optimistic. Are not convicted murderers buried coffinless and in quick-lime after the hanging? Let us give up these time-consuming jests. Here are your alternatives to Mrs Collins and her being brought to bed. Either you left the party in order to avoid Merle Patterson, or else you left the party and she followed you out of the house by mutual arrangement so that you could discuss your private affairs.'

'I've told you before! We no longer had private affairs to discuss.'

'Miss Patterson seems to have thought you had.'

'So you expect me to choose the second alternative and agree that Merle and I had arranged to meet outside the house that night!'

'It would be wise for you to admit it.'

'Why?'

'Because I am sure it is the truth.'

'Tell me why you think so.'

'I have two reasons. For one thing, you had told Miss

Kempson-Conyers that you expected a call and would have to absent yourself at some point from the party in order to attend on Mrs Collins.'

'How does that prove anything?'

'Surely, that you knew (as Mrs Collins was a figment of your brain) you would need an excuse to get away from the party at some point and had prepared yourself with one which could not be gainsaid.'

'And your second point?'

'It depends upon the first. You knew that Miss Patterson had arranged with her brother that she should take his place. You had thought that she would still be in the car when you met and it upset the plan a little when the unsuspecting Mrs Kempson invited her into the house. You managed, I expect, to speak to Miss Patterson while Amabel and her grandmother were still occupied in greeting the guests who were continuing to arrive. Miss Patterson proposed a new plan, which was that, after the pretended call was supposed to have come through, she should go into the garden at the first opportunity and that you two should hold your conclave in her car, as you had arranged.'

'Well, all right, fair enough, so far. And then?'

'I think you had a genuine call, and that it came earlier than the bogus one you had planned. I also think it was one which you did not hesitate to answer, and that, in fact, you welcomed it. You were not looking forward to your interview with Miss Patterson. You knew she would be reproachful; you thought she might be angry and even tearful, so, although you were determined to return to the party in the hope of having a lovers' meeting, however short, with Amabel Kempson-Conyers, you left it late enough to feel certain that, by the time you got back, Miss Patterson would have taken her three companions back to London and you would be spared an embarrassing interview.'

'And so?'

'You came back to find that Merle Patterson had gone out into the grounds, as arranged, but had not come back. A search-party was organised, her body was found and there was no doubt that she had been murdered. In other words, she had kept the tryst which, because of circumstances unforeseen by you, but of which you were quick to take advantage, you had managed to avoid.'

'I didn't kill her. I swear I didn't. I mean, you don't kill girls because they are prepared to make nuisances of themselves.'

'No? Perhaps you are not as well acquainted with the records of criminal behaviour as I am. Girls and women have been murdered simply because they were in the way. Have you heard of Emily Kaye?—of Ellen Warder?—of Harriet Staunton?—of Mrs Armstrong?—of Belle Elmore, as Mrs Crippen called herself professionally? I could go on. Shall I do so?'

'But Merle *wasn't* in my way! I had finished with her and she knew it. I admit I was a bit of a heel where she was concerned. She told me so in letters, anyway. I also admit I never intended to meet her in the grounds that night. I had nothing to say to her. The call I was planning to receive was just a myth, as you say. I intended to leave the house and drive off. I usually ride a horse in the village, but I use Doctor Matters' car at times and always after dark. Anyway, any double-cross act I'd planned with Merle proved unnecessary. A genuine call came through and I made the most of it.'

'Ah, yes, the genuine call. Tell me about that.'

'It came from Doctor Matters. I shouldn't criticise him to outsiders, I suppose, but he really is the most frightful old ass and to my mind completely gaga. He rang up to say that as I'd borrowed the car I was to go at once to the Pratts' house—he gave me the address—and tell them he'd given a wrong prescription and that if they'd already been to the chemist with it, Mrs Pratt was on no account to touch the stuff, but to bring it to the surgery next morning.'

'And this errand took you out of the party at an early stage in the proceedings?'

'Yes. I went off at once, of course. You can't play about with dangerous drugs.'

'And you were absent for nearly four hours?'

'Well, not as long as that.'

'Doctor Tassall, I refuse to credit your story. For one thing, Doctor Matters does his own dispensing. He does not issue prescriptions to be handed in at chemists' shops. Furthermore, it could not possibly have taken you all that time to perform such an errand. Doctor Matters' practice would have to extend to the other side of the County if it had. For your own sake, tell me the truth. I will be plain with you. If I could believe that you had any reason for disposing of Mr Ward, I would subscribe to your immediate arrest, but, so far as I know, you had no motive for that. All the same, you did have a motive for murdering Miss Patterson and doctors have committed murder before this. Come, now. For all we know at present, there may be two murderers in this village and there is nothing, so far, to show that you are not one of them.'

He shrugged his shoulders and decided to make the best of it.

'Oh, well, if you must have it,' he said, 'as I say, I never intended to meet Merle for a showdown. It couldn't do any good. I'd arranged with one of the chaps at the medical school to call me. I'd bought those lizard costumes from him, so I knew he'd oblige me. I had a few dances with Amabel under the disapproving eye of Mrs Kempson, then the chap's call came through. It was an invitation to join a gang of students in a rather low pub in the town. We had a few drinks and then I went back to the chap's room with two or three of the others and we played cards and had a few more drinks until I realised that Merle must have given up and gone home. The Kempson and Conyers tribe would be in bed, I thought, and a clod aimed at Amabel's window would bring her to the front door.'

'Instead of which, you found yourself pulled in to assist in the search for Miss Patterson. I cannot understand why you did not come out with this story at the beginning. Surely you realised that it gave you an alibi for the time of Miss Patterson's death?'

'I didn't realise at first that I needed an alibi. I'd committed myself to this story about being called out to a maternity case and I thought Amabel and her people, especially Mrs

Kempson, would take a very dim view if they knew I'd left the birthday party to go on a toot with the lads. I couldn't have let Amabel know, either, that I'd agreed to a tête-à-tête with Merle out in the grounds. You know what girls are. She'd have thought it was—she'd have thought I was double-crossing her, and that would have been the end of everything.'

I felt that I had the truth from him at last. It remained to check his alibi and this I have done. There is no doubt in my mind that, whatever happened in the case of Mr Ward, young Doctor Tassall had no part in the murder of Merle Patterson unless the medical evidence respecting the time of her death was hopelessly out.

This left me with one obvious suspect, but there were difficulties. Only if we could prove that Nigel Kempson had mistaken Merle Patterson for Lionel Kempson-Conyers did his guilt appear even possible, but it made the death of Mr Ward rather less unaccountable. However, we still had to find the reason, if there was one, for Nigel to want to kill either of them. In no way could he hope to inherit the Hill Manor estate, so it was not possible to determine how the child's death could benefit him. The same fact applied in the case of Mr Ward, even if Nigel had believed that the man who had been murdered was the rightful heir.

All the same, even though the photographer had proved a broken reed in that he had lied about waiting for Nigel to pick him up outside the cinema, it was necessary to reconsider Nigel's statement that he had arrived at the pick-up point and hung about there in his car for about an hour before returning to Hill House.

As in the case of Doctor Tassall, there was a time-lag to be taken into account. To pick up the photographer at eleven, Nigel would need to leave Hill House at least not later than ten-forty. At that time Mrs Kempson was in bed, her daughter and son-in-law had retired to their own quarters, Doctor Tassall had been called away and Merle Patterson was still in the house.

As (presumably) Nigel could not have known that Merle had made an appointment to meet Tassall out in the grounds, he could have mistaken her for Lionel and killed her when he met her on his return. If this had been the case, he might not have gone to the town at all, since, according to the medical evidence, Merle could not have died later than about eleven o'clock and it would have been impossible for him to have driven to town, waited for even the shortest time outside the cinema and returned to the grounds of the manor by eleven.

If he had not attempted to keep the appointment with the photographer, it was necessary to find out what he *had* been doing, since he had not actually come back into the house until well after midnight.

The obvious explanation was that he had been burying Mr Ward's body, but that brought me up against the brick wall which had been a so far insurmountable obstacle throughout the whole enquiry. If Nigel had buried Mr Ward, the inference needs must be that he had killed him. But why? Nobody except Mrs Kempson had anything to gain by Ward's death, and even her gain would only be the saving of a few miserable pounds a week which she could well spare. There seemed no *sense* in Mr Ward's death, and that, my dear Sir Walter, intrigued me vastly.

To whom, I asked myself for perhaps the hundredth time, was Mr Ward such a menace that, at whatever risk, he had to be removed? The only answer which has suggested itself so far is that he might have become a menace to the first Mr Ward, the mysterious figure who had appeared upon the Hill House scene five years earlier and then must have disappeared within a matter of days, only to be impersonated by the second (and subsequently murdered) Mr Ward.

I placed the matter before the inspector.

'We can be pretty certain Kempson did not show up outside the cinema that night,' he said.

'Upon the now completely false evidence of the photographer?'

'No. We've got two witnesses, quite unbiased, both of them. One is the commissionaire at the cinema who states he was on duty there until after the place closed down at eleven, and the other is our man on the beat. They both swear that no car was parked outside or even reasonably near the cinema up to eleven-fifteen that night. The commissionaire went off duty when the cinema closed down, but my chap was up and down all the time, on and off, until midnight, and there was no parked car. I took their statements separately and there's no doubt about it. Wherever Kempson went that night, he did not turn up outside that cinema.'

I went back to my notebooks, beginning with the first letter I had received from Mrs Kempson and continuing with all the jottings I had made subsequent to that. It was then that the truth not only dawned on me, but did so in a kind of sunburst. The identity of the first Mr Ward was no longer a mystery. Once I realised that, the rest of the puzzle fell into place as certainly as the apparently unpredictable ball at the roulette table falls into its mysteriously appointed compartment and stakes are won and lost at one and the same time. I was certain of the identity of the criminal and I did not think there would be much difficulty in proving it.

Mrs Kempson's first letter and later remarks were helpful up to a point. She was doubtful whether the man who had claimed to be her brother was, in fact, Ward, yet there was something about his voice which appeared to be familiar to her.

She was determined to secure the inheritance for her grandson, but she also had not quite a clear conscience with regard to Ward, even though he had declared himself an emulator of Esau and was prepared to forfeit his inheritance for a mess or pottage.

All the same, it has been shown, since the two murders, that both the Mr Wards were impostors and that the real Mr Ward died in America before he had a chance of claiming the Hill Manor estate.

Only two points still needed to be worked out, but I had considered them before and I felt that I had positive answers to both of them. There was the question of the time-lag once again. In the case of young Tassall and Nigel Kempson it was a matter of hours, hours which I felt I could now account for, but in the case of the first Mr Ward there was an interval of five years to be bridged.

There was also the question of the substitution of the first Mr Ward by the second Mr Ward, a change unsuspected by either Mrs Landgrave, who had never seen the first one, or Mrs Kempson who, by her own choice, had never set eyes on the second one while he was alive.

The explanations I could find to fit in with my theories were that, during the five years' time-lag, somebody had been making either overt or disguised attempts to get Mrs Kempson to change the terms of her will. The most likely person to have so employed his time was Nigel Kempson. With regard to the substitution, it seemed that it must have been necessary to have a Mr Ward at Mrs Landgrave's, since otherwise Mrs Kempson might find out that her monthly money orders were not being cashed. As for Mr Ward's lodgings, the Landgraves, as I summed them up, were certainly not the people to take money for a non-existent lodger.

The inference was that the first Mr Ward was known elsewhere and it was necessary for him to appear in his usual haunts, a thought which had occurred to me earlier, but not in connexion with Nigel.

Again I went over my notes. Then I turned up Mrs Kempson's letters to me, and there it all was. The voice she had heard before; the discussion she had had with Nigel and they agreed that Mr Ward should receive thirty thousand pounds at her death in consideration of his abandoning all claim to the estate; the substitution of another Mr Ward as Mrs Landgrave's lodger, since Nigel himself had a lucrative position and had to be in London most of his time; his mother an actress and his father possibly an actor, so that he was able to play the part of the first Mr Ward without arousing more than the dimmest of doubts in Mrs Kempson's mind; the untidy moustache; the pince-nez; most of all, the gloves.

This all seemed obvious enough, but it still did not account for the two murders. A prime factor, I decided, was the mental deterioration of the second Mr Ward. Nigel must have wondered whether there would come a point when this individual (probably an ex-criminal whom Nigel had promised to help) would give the game away. There was also a possibility that he had been in no wise as crazy as his conduct would suggest, but had tried his hand at a little mild blackmail, for, to some extent, Nigel must have been obliged to take him into his confidence.

This could explain the first murder, but it still did not account for the death of Merle Patterson. The reason for that remained speculative, but I thought I knew the answer.

The police were certain that the girl had not been killed down by the sheepwash where her body was found. Neither they nor I had ever really believed that, dressed as she was, she would have strayed so far from the house. There was, however, the distinct possibility that, believing Doctor Tassall to have been called away on a genuine case, she had gone as far as the lodge gates to meet him on his return.

There somebody had dragged her inside the deserted lodge and killed her. My theory was that this was because she had come upon Nigel humping the body of the second Mr Ward out of the lodge where he had hidden it after he had killed his understudy on the previous day, having first enticed him up to the house, on what pretext I cannot say.

Of course, all this was mere speculation, and the only way or proving it, it seemed to me, was to confront Nigel with such evidence as we had, accuse him to his face and find out whether he could refute the accusation. The reason for his lengthy absence from the birthday party was a factor to take into account. He had two dead bodies to dispose of. He transported both by car, I think. He was to have picked up the photographer in a car, you will remember. I think he drove first straight down Lovers' Lane and put the girl's body, with the fancy costume torn to pieces, beside the sheepwash in the hope that the gypsies would be credited with the crime, as, at the very beginning, one of them was—and indeed he might well have been convicted—but for the intervention of the two children and the evidence supplied by their uncle.

Then Nigel returned for Mr Ward's body. He knew where

to hide it, for young Lionel Kempson-Conyers who, according to the Clifton children, 'always blabbed', could have told him about the grave-like hole in the floor of the ruined cottage. It was sheer bad luck—if one can call it bad luck when a murderer is hoist, so to speak, with his own petard—that the children should have had sufficient curiosity regarding the filled-in hole to get the poor village idiot to dig it out for them, and that Mrs Winter knew the sound of his car.

You may ask why, having, in his capacity as the first Mr Ward, assured himself of thirty thousand pounds under the terms of Mrs Kempson's will, Nigel did not add her murder to his tally. I think he had genuine feeling for her and was willing to wait for her death from natural causes. Because of the difference in their ages he probably thought that he would not have to wait very long. Like other murderers I have met, he was by no means altogether bad.

Of course, sooner or later he would still have had to dispose of the second Mr Ward had that unfortunate man remained sane, but I think he had planned to do that after Mrs Kempson's death. Then he would have presented himself to the lawyers in his disguise as the first Mr Ward and claimed his thirty thousand pounds.

CHAPTER 19

Margaret and Kenneth

So it was poor Nigel Kempson after all, although I do not know why I still think of him with compassion. He was a double murderer and he had killed an entirely innocent, although I think a very silly, lovesick young girl as well as the madman we knew as Mr Ward.

Mrs Lestrange Bradley (Dame Beatrice as she became later on) got our address from Aunt Kirstie and came to see us in our London home to tell us all about it. She said that our discovery of Mr Ward's body when Kenneth thought we were getting Poachy to dig for buried treasure had been of great help to the police, but that did not comfort us very much. The only good thing about it all, so far as I could see, was that they did not hang Nigel. He went shooting rabbits on Lye Hill and accidentally or purposely shot himself before he could be arrested. I think he realised that Mrs Bradley was getting at the truth.

I suppose thirty thousand pounds is a great deal of money, especially if you compare it with the five thousand which was all that Nigel stood to obtain in his own name under Mrs Kempson's will, but, on thinking it over, I do not really believe that the late Mr Kempson had made any stipulation as to how his wife was to leave the money when she died.

I think she believed that Nigel was Mr Kempson's own illegitimate son whom he had never had the courage to acknowledge and, although she loved Nigel in her possessive way, largely because she was so lonely with her husband dead and her only daughter abroad most of the time, I imagine that she resented and never forgave her husband's infidelity (if unfaithful he had been) and for that reason she refused to have Nigel legally adopted, which might have given him a title to the estate or, at any rate, a substantial share in the late Mr Kempson's fortune. Instead, he was to be left a beggarly five thousand pounds instead of the sum which no doubt he felt he had a right to expect.

For how long he had planned to impersonate Mrs Kempson's brother Ward it is impossible to say, but, of course, it could not have been before Mrs Kempson received the news of Ward's death.

So what Mrs Bradley calls 'the first Mr Ward' made his appearance and (possibly again to vent her spite against her dead husband, so strangely are people constituted) Mrs Kempson told Nigel that she was leaving her 'brother' thirty thousand pounds, little knowing that her beneficiary was the other party to the agreement.

It was the last holiday we ever spent in Hill village, for our grandfather died that winter, all the property was sold up and the aunts and Uncle Arthur moved away. However, we were given bicycles the following summer and father cycled with us to visit his relations in another part of Oxfordshire.

One day we decided to cycle to Hill on our own, but when we came to the culvert which led on to The Marsh, Kenneth said:

'I don't believe I want to go any further.'

'Well, let's spend our money at Mother Honour's,' I said, 'and then go back. Other people will be in Aunt Kirstie's and grandfather's, so it wouldn't be fun. Even the hermit's cottage isn't there any more. Look! Do you see? They've pulled it down. Do you believe there was ever any treasure hidden in it?'

'I did when I was younger,' said Kenneth.

VINTAGE